Scot Poet
D914
£8.50

Crumbs of Love

Novels by Hunter Steele

McCandy
The Wishdoctor's Song
Chasing the Gilded Shadow
Lord Hamlet's Castle
The Lords of Montplaisir

for my father
Mungo Steele

and for Karel
who helped
make it happen

crumbs of love

Lyrics, 1965–90

Hunter Steele

with three appendices
on the use of verse and music
in education

and illustrations by
Mary Ruth Craig

BLACK ACE BOOKS

First published in 1992 by
Black Ace Books
Duns, TD11 3SG, Scotland

© Hunter Steele 1992
Lyrics © Maran Steele Music 1992
Original illustrations © Mary Ruth Craig 1992
Typography © Black Ace Editorial 1992

Typeset in Scotland by Black Ace Editorial

Printed in Great Britain by Martin's The Printers
Berwick Upon Tweed, TD15 1RS

All rights reserved. Strictly except for the non-profit-making educational and charitable uses specified in the introduction, or in conformity with the provisions of the Copyright Act 1956 (as amended), no part of this book may be reprinted or reproduced or exploited in any form or by any electronic, mechanical or other means, whether such means be known now or invented hereafter, including photocopying, or text capture by optical character recognition, or in any information storage or retrieval system, without permission in writing from the publishers. Any person or organization committing any unauthorized act in relation to this publication may be liable to criminal prosecution and civil action for damages. Hunter Steele is identified as author of this work in accordance with Section 77 of the Copyright, Designs and Patents Act 1988.

A CIP catalogue record for this book
is available from the British Library

ISBN   1-872988-02-4

The author and publishers gratefully acknowledge
subsidy from the Scottish Arts Council
towards the publication of this volume

CONTENTS

List of Illustrations	8
Introduction	9

PART I, LATER 1960s
Lyrics	14
Story – 'White Christmas'	36

PART II, EARLIER 1970s
Lyrics	40
Story – 'A Song for Atlantis'	71

PART III, LATER 1970s
Lyrics	84
Faction – 'The Philosopher's Mother'	112

PART IV, EARLIER 1980s
Lyrics	116
Story – 'The Asbestos Factory'	135

PART V, LATER 1980s
Lyrics	144

APPENDICES
I – Verse in education	164
II – Creating lyrics	169
III – Working with music	180

REFERENCE
Suggested reading	187
Index of titles by page number	188
Index of titles by alphabet	190
About Black Ace Books	192

ILLUSTRATIONS

crumbs of love – frontalpiece   4

FOR LYRIC TITLED

the night is kind	28
go your way	35
leaves	43
the serpent caper	50
prayer from the trees	56
graven faces	68
the emperor and the geisha girl	88
soapsuds in my gravy (tentacles)	95
looking forward to summer	103
moonlight shines	109
Lady Lovely & Mr Teddy Bear	123
the cipher	131
love is lonely	149
light a candle to the lonely	153
Hannah's beautiful day	158

Introduction

Not all song lyrics read well as verse. Mine are no exception, and one (which nearly became a hit single in Germany) has a chorus consisting mainly of 'do be do be do . . . ' – after the hackneyed Sartre/Sinatra joke. It works as a recording, but I would shudder to see it alone in print. Many good – certainly, many successful – songs have feeble lyrics. But so what?

Mediocre novels are often turned into better movies, and the weakness of the novel is no reason to condemn the movie. But just as one may decline to read the novel, either before or after the movie, so one may feel no pressing need to read 'I love you, baby, please don't go, rock me, yeah!' umpteen times in book anthology form.

So one criterion for the present selection is that each lyric should have sufficient – albeit modest – poetic interest (in structure, form, content . . .) to be read as well as heard.

Some songs, like young and fruity wines, are divine at the time but date alarmingly quickly. One of mine was about a girl who had 'Eyes Like Steve McQueen'. This, sadly, would now be in poor taste, and before long it would become meaningless. So . . . all such lyrics have been excluded.

Another principle of selection has been authenticity. I have always liked the story about the art critic who asks Picasso whether a certain painting is genuine. Picasso squints at the canvas casually, and says:

'It's a fake.'

'But, maestro,' the jubilant critic pounces, 'I saw you paint this one with my own eyes!'

'*Et alors?*' scoffs Picasso. 'I often paint fakes.'

Similarly, songwriters – even talented ones – often rustle up fakes, especially when under pressure to supply new product to service their recording contracts. I too have written fakes, sometimes out of greed, sometimes boredom, sometimes desperation – form without content; sentiment without emotion; ultimately, paint without walls – and I have tried to banish such fakes from this collection. However, this is where self-deception may already have crept in, so the final verdict on authenticity rests, as always, with you – the consumer.

But who is the consumer? Who wants a book of lyrics? What use is it?

I certainly hope these verses will give pleasure, but this book is also offered for practical purposes.

I have frequently been in teaching situations – children in schools, foreign students learning English, undergraduates wanting to become songwriters – where it has been useful to draw on a store of singable lyrics whose original tunes are unknown to the students. It might be thought that the world is full of such lyrics, but my finding is that it isn't. Shakespeare's sonnets are incomparable, but not very singable or . . . current. The same goes for T. S. Eliot's *Waste Land* (if not *Practical Cats*), and so on. Bob Dylan, Paul Simon and Leonard Cohen have written some rather good lyrics, but their tunes are also world-famous, and impossible to think away from the words.

So, for my own past teaching purposes, I have used my own lyrics. (Some suggestions as to classroom applications are given in appendices at the end of this book.) If other educationists now wish to use them similarly, they are welcome to do so. My catalogue is not owned by Paul McCartney. It is owned by my own company, and we hereby give general authorization for any performance undertaken for non-profit-making educational purposes. Thus, you may sing without fear of pursuit by the Performing Right Society, or the Music Publishers' Association. (Please note, however, that photocopying rights are administered in the usual way by the ALCS: the Authors' Licensing and Collecting Society. In any case, if you'd rather work with multiple copies of the book, than go to the trouble of making yet more ozonogenic photocopies, Black Ace Books will offer you a tempting educational discount.)

The overriding requirement, then, is that these lyrics be *singable*, and this is guaranteed by the fact that they all have been sung – some to several melodies. My own best settings are passable, but my musical achievement is limited by the range of my voice, and I am well aware that many composers can produce more memorable musical results than I usually do. If, on the commercial front, other songwriters wish to turn these lyrics into million-selling songs, that's fine by me. The only qualifications are that you and your publisher get half, I and my company get half, and the permission is non-exclusive: you acquire no rights over the same lyrics as used in other settings.

So much for commercialese, but what about subject-matter?

I once asked a group of exceptionally intelligent students, aged between eighteen and twenty-five and of nationalities from Brazil to Japan, why more songs were not written about the Dow Jones Index. This kindled a lively debate which evolved towards a consensus that the Dow Jones Index is not of urgent interest to most persons who write songs and buy records. Or, as my favourite philosopher – Schopenhauer – puts it:

'We are accustomed to see the poets mainly concerned with describing the love of the sexes. This is as a rule the chief theme of all dramatic works, tragical as well as comical, romantic as well as classical, Indian as well as European. Not less is it the material of by far the largest part of lyrical, and also of epic poetry . . . '

Madonna might phrase it in words of fewer letters, but the sexual-love preoccupation is the same. Since song is simple, and a natural first art form for young people to appreciate and experiment with, it is hardly surprising that the basic statements are limited:

> *I love you.*
> *Please love me.*
> *You are my everything.*
> *I couldn't live without you.*
> *Please don't go.*
> *Why did you deceive/leave me?*

Many popular songs consist, lyrically, of nothing but such bald single lines repeated over and over. That doesn't doom them to failure, of course, since it's not what you sing that counts, it's how you sing it.

My own lyrics are probably just as obsessed with sex/love as most, but there are also several which border on what some might call The Spiritual. Perhaps I should stress, though, that the 'god' and 'angels' in such earlier songs have less to do with the Church of Scotland Santa than with Alan Watts and mystic chemistry.

A third cluster addresses ecological issues: overpopulation, deforestation; pollution of the oceans. Some of these lyrics are over twenty years old, but they seem more relevant today than ever. If any charity such as Friends of the Earth or Greenpeace sees a fund-generating use for lyrics like 'Soapsuds In My Gravy' and 'The Trees They Did Grow High', please get in touch, and permission will almost certainly be granted. (The reason we can't issue a blanket licence, here, is that [eg] Cambridge University Press is also a registered charity.)

The lyrics that follow appear not by subject but, loosely, by date of birth. The five sections correspond to the five half-decades from the mid 1960s to the later 1980s. To punctuate the verse, each of the first four sections concludes with a short story relating to the same period. There has been some shuffling of the lyrics, for aesthetic and typographical reasons, but psychologists of aging may rest assured that, broadly, the songs in Part I were written in the author's late teens, and the lyrics in Part V in his thirties. Whether this exhibits any progression, or decline, from innocence to experience, optimism to pessimism, McEwan's Export to Côtes du Rhône Villages . . . I trepidate to hypothesize. While Schopenhauer observes:

'If Petrarch's passion had been satisfied, his song would have been silenced from that time forth, like that of the bird, as soon as the eggs are laid.'

Finally, much thanks. To everyone I have ever fallen in love with. And vice versa. To my goddaughters, Hannah and Rachel, and to everyone who will fall in love with them. To Mary Ruth Craig, for her fine illustrations. To Mike Ryan, for his software magic. To Cairns Craig, for his liberal vision. To those co-writers with whom I have worked over the years, particularly Mike Maran and Carrie Steingold, who have often strengthened my lyrics by scrapping weak lines, restructuring refrains, etc – for songwriting often works best as a collaboration, and a good lyric can frequently be improved by the surgery of a versatile composer.

And to Boo, for the sunshine.

H.S., Duns, Summer 1992

Part I

LATER 1960s

not for you

you left me by the silver stream
like something pawned to be redeemed
you had so many foreign lands to see
like France and Spain, maybe Italy
you'd rather see the world than me

> the world won't change that much you know
> oh, my love, what made you go?

you treat me like the stream so clear
always changing but always there
but I'm like a bird on the garden wall
I'm like a leaf on the tree so tall
when summer goes the leaf must fall

and now the autumn wind has blown
the leaf has fallen and the bird has flown
don't try to find which way he flew
when you come home in a month or two
I'll still be here but not for you

light and laughter

I'm a lucky man
I got a hundred nothings in my hand
other people plough and sow
I just watch my nothings grow
when they're ripe and when I'm old
I will see them turn to gold

> light and laughter
> are my seeds
> and I grow them
> wild like weeds
> take some laughter
> take some light
> you need never
> fear the night

I got a bird on a silken string
going to teach that bird to sing
when I've taught her all I know
she will break the string and go
but I know that when she's gone
through the world she'll sing my song

I don't wear a ball and chain
drive a car or fly a plane
most times I don't move at all
except when I'm drunk I sometimes crawl
I see my nothings growing fast
and I think maybe my luck will last

the monday boy

it's only a monday
he's only a monday's child
hollow-eyed, and he cannot hide
for there's nothing
to hide behind

      take him out
      and bury him deep
      in the snow

heed not the cold now
heed not the cold and the pain
his lips are numb, his words won't come
and the monday boy
dies by no name

soon he'll be gone now
soon will come peace for a while
just bury him deep
in the cold, cold snow
and wait for spring

the ballad of the galleon

all on the ocean floor
I lie alone
all alone
I lie
half buried in the sand
seaweed clothes my bones
clothes my bones
in the sand
and deep within my womb
my mermaids sleep
mermaids sleep, in my womb

all around my bones
rainbow fishes play
fishes play
round my bones
and bound within my hold
New Spanish treasures lie
treasures lie
in my hold
while miles above my head
those sailing ships go by
they go by, o'er my head

but my world is still and dark
my mermaids I can't see
I can't see
in the dark
still Neptune guards my grave
that I may rest in peace
rest in peace
in my grave
so here I will remain
intruders all will die
all will die, and I remain

spiders

spider I
spinning my thread
weaving a fine web
to capture the woman
I love

much did I spin
long did I wait
praying this woman
would enter my beautiful
snare

but my love's no fly
she's like the wind
took a big breath
and blew my poor fine web
away

spider she
biding her time
takes what she wants
from the lover she then
will destroy

sleepy eyes

big brown eyes
that recently
were open wide
and so alive
are sleepy now

lips I know
that spoke so much
not long ago
and kissed me so
are silent now

smile I see
those lips are curling
sleepily
so soft for me
but resting now

sleepy-eyes
wants me to sing
a lullaby
well, close your eyes
and I'll sing you
to sleep

still the winds

every day the mirror changes
forms, dissolves and rearranges
colours pastel, colours fair
gleam of teeth and glint of hair
many colours, many shades
each one glows and quickly fades
turning black and white to grey
and leaving me my mirror
rearranged to face another day

all the time the river rumbles
laughs and plays and onwards tumbles
once and always past the fir trees
old and new as mother earth is
many rivers, light and free
born and dying constantly
hearing the sea and answering her call
and giving me one river
made from others yet more than them all

in the winter deep in snow
build a snowman, watch him grow
coat and muffler for his clothes
bits of coal his eyes and nose
let the storms of winter rage
see the snowman quickly age
changing his appearance every day
but faithfully still standing
till the snow has melted all away

through the fingers of my hands
bright jewels fall like grains of sand
much too rich am I to care
I walk on diamonds everywhere
times I stop and stand quite still
still the winds my cup do fill
treasures at my feet just seem to fall
and quietly I am grateful
prizing nothing while I worship all

thistledown

everywhere I go
I see apples ripe on apple trees
but people only want the leaves
and them they burn
and them they burn

every girl I know
either wants a priceless gown
or else to be like thistledown
so that she
may fly away

all around me now
I see red and gold and green
I hear guitars and tambourines
and I feel the wind
blowing round me all day long
drowning out my loudest songs
and with such ease
oh, with such ease

grotto motto

wherever you tread
tread lightly
tread lightly
or you might stir up
clouds of dust
clouds you can't get through

    lightly as you go
    and take the corners slow

wherever you tread
tread lightly
tread lightly
else you might waken
sleeping dogs
and you just might get chewed

I love Elizabeth

I love Elizabeth
I love Elizabeth
does she love me?
when she's away from me
in some far colony
does she still pray for me?
does she love me?

she loves another man
she loves another man
does he love her?
does he get through to her?
give her what's due to her?
always stay true to her?
does he love her?

the garden

among the weeds a flower dies
her petals fade and fall
rose without a thorn
daughter of the dawn
defiled by lust
returned to dust
unto the earth recalled
while all the time
green ivy climbs
the wall

then comes the gardener anxiously
to clear the weeds away
brown eyes and fingers green
pray to a power unseen
oh, wondrous lord
make sharp my sword
make strong my arm this day
yet while he stands
the gardener's hands
turn grey

as ages pass there comes a lamb
unto the gardener's tomb
the weeds grow helpless and green
the lamb grows fevered and lean
unhappy weeds
consumed by greed
to be by greed consumed
but more than that
the lamb grows fat
the garden sinks in gloom

the gondolier

lady, you don't have to steer
let me be your gondolier
I'll take you there
through the dark canals of night
we will journey with delight
I your lowly gondolier
and you my fare

pilot of the waterways
I call the sea to send you praise
upon the air
midnight song from the open sea
play my lady your melody
sound her name and tease her ears
smile on her

other boats of every kind
we will pass and leave behind
as we speed on
pass beneath the bridge of sighs
touch the walls on either side
on then to the great lagoon
we'll be there soon

no other boatman ventures here
the waters wear a calm veneer
until the dawn
shirt of crimson silk for me
my love wears a memory
bring her joy for years to come
keep her warm

the last winter

know that the hills are high
know that the hills are high
and you who would climb them are lame
a bird that can't fly, you are lame
for a time
know that the hills are high

know that the soldiers are gone
know that the soldiers are gone
there's no one left here to kill
but for me, and they leave me alone
to die very soon
know that the soldiers are gone

know that the soldiers won't come
know that the soldiers won't come
all the eagles have flown
and you may rest safe in my home
till I die
know that the soldiers won't come

know that the hills are green
know that the hills are green
by springtime you will be well
the hillside berries will swell
and we will move on
know that the hills are green

the railway

late in the evening
well after the sun went down
a lady came a-walking by
asking me to take her
to the railway line

> *I'll take you there*
> *but there's nothing much left to see*
> *sleepers lie in silent rows*
> *the station has long since been closed*
> *no train will come this way again*

oh no, she told me
what you say is not true
my man comes on the midnight train
take me to the station
let me wait for him

> *I'll take you there*
> *and you'll see I do not lie*
> *cobwebs in the waiting room*
> *no light shines within the gloom*
> *no train will come this way again*

she went in, she waited
she waited till the morning came
morning came, but still no train
how long would you wait on
if you were her?

> *no train*
> *I tell you no train will come*
> *can't you see the line's disused?*
> *rusted rails and broken shoes*
> *no train will come this way again*

sold for a song

so I said goodbye
I'm not sure why
it's really hard to say
I have to change my style
and be free for a while
to stroll and sing all day

> to stroll and sing all day
> just to stroll and sing all day

oh, long ago
I knew I would go
but I never could say quite when
the light in my eye
for you has died
and it never will shine again

> it never will shine again
> no, it never will shine again

oh, cruel it is
to sing like this
and you can call it wrong
it may be a crime
but it's not the first time
I sold my love for a song

> I sold my love for a song
> I sold my love for a song

the night is kind

only so
your eyes may shine
light I now
and leave burning
all the night
this candle flame
so feel no shame
the night is kind
to lovers such
as you, and me

        the night is kind
        to lovers such
        as you, and me

turn to me
your body warm
swim with me
as fishes we will be
deep in the sea
secure
no storm to fear
no wind, no waves
as we go swimming
on and on

soon comes light
and love must hide
dim till night
like some ghost
that cannot walk by day
but know
that until dawn
your eyes will shine
your skin will glow
our love will burn

mistress, go gaily

mistress, go slowly
don't scamper so over the meadow
it doesn't go well
with your almost sorrowful eye
your eye on today
while your body remembers tomorrow
I easily see
that the hour of your leaving is nigh

> she comes to tell me goodbye, yes
> she comes to tell me goodbye

over and over
you swear that it hurts you to leave me
again and again
you say that you can't bear to go
all this you say
when you have no intention of staying
our final act
you turn into a second-rate show

> I will not miss her at all, no
> I will not miss her at all

mistress, go gaily
lay boldly your hands on tomorrow
only the clowns
and the second-hand people pretend
I feel empty a little
but nothing remotely like sorrow
I feel like I feel
when a good story comes to an end

> and I'll try and remember her name, yes
> I'll try and remember her name

water lady

stand I naked by the sea
water lady swirls round me
moaning her love
lasting forever
outliving jewels

water lady knows the joys
of ebbing and of flowing
would she trade them
for the power
of perfect silent knowing?
will she change
and always be still?

water lady, comfort me
take me in your warm body
hold me there
no-one will follow
no-one will dare

crazy days

eagerly you
ask of me
what will
tomorrow bring?
will there fall
a golden rain
to sweeten
everything
and waken the blind?

    and every day gets lazier
    every haze gets hazier
    all that you say gets crazier
    still I don't mind

you must be
a stranger still
to take me
seriously
to gaze on me
with trusting eyes
and wholly
fail to see
that I don't mind

cut the silken
threads of dreams
that bind my sleep
to me
bid the bright blue sky
swoop down
and swallow
the deep blue sea
and I won't mind

pledge of love

weariness now lays me down
and feathers fill the air
I can almost neither breathe nor see
and I almost do not care
oh, tired birds don't fly
and tired men don't change the world
tired men don't try
tired men don't love too much
tired men just die

>   yet you come close
>   with your pledge of love
>   you pledge your love
>   with your pledge of love . . .

well, who says I even want your love
and the fairy tales you tell?
who says I want the scent of you
and the beads you wear so well?
there's no way you can know
and yet it's true, I know I do
and I do not have much pride
all I want is to lie by you
and let the years go by

all I want is to lie by you
and lie by you again
all I want is to lie by you
and lie there till the end
and for us to while the world away
till only harmony remains

go your way

Once I had no wish to climb
I used to squander all my time
I used to spend it with my friends
And that's how I lost them in the end
They said

> Go your way
> Go your way
> We have no more time to spend

I told a farmer in a field
Trying to increase his yield:
'I hope your corn and turnips grow
But why you bother I don't know!'
He said

> Go your way
> Go your way
> Unless you wish to plough and sow

Then I spied the moonman on the moon
I heard him sing a moonman tune
I said: 'Mr Moonman, can I sing?
I tell you I love everything!'
He said

> Go your way
> Go your way
> This is one song you cannot sing

White Christmas

David tossed and turned in his warm winter bed. He was five, and this would be his first White Christmas. Surely. Earlier he had watched the snowflakes carpeting the stable roof, and swirling like huge white moths round the light in the yard.

Why should he suffer from toothache on Christmas Eve? Oh, how he hated his pain. More fiercely than a wasp that once had stung him for no reason. And who could be to blame but God? God who created all things? Including pain?

For a miserable hour David punished God by refusing to say his prayers. Then, throbbing with toothache and frustration, he knelt inside his bed and said the prayers his mother had taught him. Finally he asked God to forgive his bad thoughts, and to please make sure that Santa was not delayed.

Christmas to David was like a paradise island in an ocean of identical days. Last year's Christmas was the first he could remember, and often, during the year, he had made pilgrimages there: revisiting the enormous stocking Santa brought him – much bigger than himself – which later he had opened in the security of his parents' bed. After breakfast, another pile of many-coloured parcels underneath the Christmas tree. Soldiers and swords; cars and trains; bright books and jigsaw puzzles. Dinner he remembered chiefly for the Christmas pudding, its blazing holly crown, and the sweet, crunchy brandy butter of which he ate too much.

And this Christmas would be even more splendid. Everything promised that. The farmhouse was full of guests. His favourite cousins had come. His mysterious Aunt Victoria would tell them about her adventures in far-off lands. Above all: this Christmas would be White.

Yet now David's joy was soured by the awful ache in his jaw. Tears of pain and grief he let fall freely, but sobs he stifled; lest some grown-up passing his door should hear. What, he wondered miserably, did it feel like to *not* have toothache?

But he couldn't quite recall.

Earlier, to make matters worse, there had been an unhappy

betrayal. After dinner David's Uncle John had entertained the children with conjuring tricks; and David had caught him cheating. Until today he had equated conjuring and magic. Now he distinguished between them, and conjuring had lost its charm. His belief in the Land of Magic, however, remained unshaken. For that was where Rudolph and Santa lived.

And Santa was coming soon.

Suddenly David's bedroom door flew open. Jamie, his youngest cousin, burst in – his cheeks streaked by tears.

'What's wrong?' asked David.

'Come on,' wailed Jamie. 'Get up. Santa hasn't been.'

David frowned:

'It isn't time for Santa.'

'It's Christmas morning. Michael says.'

Michael was the oldest cousin. Since his voice had begun to break his two younger brothers treated his every word as gospel.

'Listen,' insisted David. 'The grown-ups are still talking.'

Jamie slammed David's door and ran downstairs to investigate.

David winced. His pain was worsening. Bands of white fire stretched between his ear and chin. Even his nose was sore.

Minutes later David's mother came in. She explained Jamie's distress. The three cousins had a room in the attic, away from the noise and lights of the lower house. Exhausted by Christmas Eve excitements, they had fallen asleep quickly and woken up only four hours later. Michael, expecting a new watch from Santa, had forgotten to wind his old clockwork watch, which had stopped at eight in the evening. So the cousins believed it must be eight on Christmas morning.

All that meant little to David. His world had shrunk into a circle of pain, and its centre was his tooth.

David's mother was a sensitive woman, compassionate and intense. Earlier she had only left when David promised his ache was easing. Now it was obviously bad again, and she took him downstairs for some aspirins to suck and a teaspoon of gin to sip. In the sitting-room he was cheerily consoled by his father and uncle, who were drinking whisky and smoking cigars. He heard his mother wish she could take his pain from him, and suffer it herself. What did she mean? Before David returned to bed he checked the coffee-table by the fire, to see that Santa's cocoa and sandwiches had not been touched by greedy grown-ups. What a pity, he thought, that Santa's cocoa would be cold, on a night so wintry white.

Back in his room David's mother read to him from *A Christmas Carol*. When she was sure he was asleep, she closed the book and tiptoed out.

David's pain was ebbing now, but wakefulness clung to him like a limpet; the harder he tried to sleep, the wider awake he became.

Later, when his mother brought his stocking, she knelt by his bed and prayed, silently, that David would enjoy his first White Christmas. David did not see her. His eyes were screwed tight shut, for fear that Santa would vanish if he caught you spying.

Still, thought David, was it not strange that Santa arrived by the bedroom door, not the chimney, and smelling faintly of a lady's perfume?

Part II

EARLIER 1970s

playback

the soft aside
the smart reply
the tale of woe
to wet the eye
I've heard them before

okay, they're true
they're still for real
and yet they're limp
like apple peel
and they mean no more

      and no more do your gestures
      your graces and postures
      your air of being one who knows
      who tranquilly shrugs off her clothes
      and always knows a trick that's new
      that's always something else to do
      that's all okay so long as you
      can realize
      there's nothing to prove

steal the plan
you lose the man
so try and find me
if you can
for you've stolen mine

all the power
you thought was real
was only really
power to steal
and now you will find

      that you have stolen all there was
      that now there's neither plan nor cause
      that now there's neither cause nor man
      try and steal one if you can
      though you may think you see me
      it's only an effigy
      that's left to you from brighter days
      and like a tape it sometimes plays
      in mockery of what's away
      and all it very really says
      is, as you know
      there's nothing to prove

leaves

leaves that fall
as seasons call
know they when
a sad man sings

a sad man dreams
but seldom sings
a sad man dreams
that he wears wings
that he can fly
and never die
that things are other
than they are

a sad man sings
a sad man's song
a sad man sings
but not for long
for he well knows
how sadness grows
and every happy song
is a lie

the sad man loves
all things that breathe
the sad man loves
the falling leaves
and prays that they
some day all may
live easy
in a frozen world

the sad man sings
a sad man's song
and still the leaves
come falling down
falling, falling
falling
down

ice

facts you say will be known
how the cultured foods will be grown
when the test-tube babies are born
and the seeds of the ice have been sown
and sunlight has gone
it's really not worth a song
and my fingers are cold

just see how the ice cracks the wall
how the ice climbs the waterfall
oh, see how the ice claims all
and feel how the ice is cold
make me warm
and when the feasting is done
leave me a bone

the title

I have many memories
of you my love refusing
you spurned the love
a boy would share
you killed with words
a young man's care
you bid him take
his love elsewhere

why then lately in your eyes
do I detect accusing?
now I another
love embrace?
return with warmth
her heart's caress?
are your refusals
swayed by this?

angels in my dreams
pause and ask me questions
whose body
wears fine clothes for me
whose heart
holds a rose for me
whose being
makes me glad to be

who shall I say
answers this description?
who comes first
in these affairs?
is the title
yours or hers?
again I say
the choice is yours

god's tears

sailing ship upon the blue sea
I feel him reaching for me
I go walking by the blue sea
I feel you walking by me
fix your gaze upon the blue sky
look out there
look out for god's eye
count god's tears
as they whisper by
and wish him eager as we
who on his sea
are soon to be
who see a flame growing
deep in every wave
and start to sing, and wonder
what forces bring such change alive

we're the ship upon the blue sea
we'll dry god's eye with our sail
we're all ships that ever could be
and all winds that ever prevail
we're a solid ring of red fire
we burn high
put light to god's eye
tend ourselves
that we may not die
we sail wherever we will
as reasons come
and seasons call
for in every autumn
winter, spring and summer
sailing is burning
and burning is being all

you're the seasons, I am the wind
I blow to bring you to me
I am the shore and you are the sea
I feel you wash around me
we're all worlds that ever take fire
we don't die
forever we fly
wish god well
and bid him goodbye
thanks to the tears he has sown
I feel you now
and you feel me

now we're alone
god's tears are grown
become as one
you have me to tend your flame
and on me still
the waves and the seasons fall

cargo

I'm loading at your harbour
I'm laden with your cargo
in such a hold
something must yield
and all my dreams
go overboard

oh, if it's you that sleeps with me
then take charge of the memory
and pardon me my cruelty
but I believe you're lonely
for it's not me
that sleeps with you
it's just a sometime
friend of mine

and I believe he's dying
hard hit by an overload
I believe I chained him
to some dreams
that recently
went overboard

so I set your cargo down
I hope you find a lover soon

the serpent caper

one fine day
up from the sea
a green serpent came coiling
and he crawled up to me
and what did he say?

>   *help me*
>   *oh, please shelter me*
>   *for the sunlight burns my scales*

why don't you crawl
on back to the sea
slide beneath the waves
and never bother me?
and what did he say?

>   *I would gladly*
>   *do that thing*
>   *but I can't because the water boils*

oh, well that's a shame
who can be to blame?
come on look around
and point him out to me
and we'll make him pay
accordingly
we'll take away his property
we'll put him where he ought to be . . .

and then if you agree
we'll nail him to a tree
we'll finish him
but not until
we'd made him clean
and cool the sea
and what did he say?

> *your offer is most kind*
> *except it's you*
> *that's made the waters boil*

whereon I could see
how things must really be
this crazy serpent
had it in for me
so I made him pay
accordingly
I chased him off my property
and put him where he ought to be
I cut him into three
and I threw him in the sea
and I hope and pray
that from now on
he will not bother me

the omen

you come from the sky
all feathered and grey
like an omen of war
like a dealer of cold
from some northern shore
and you ask with your eyes
oh, what are these rags
that I wear?

I say my body's a toy
that I offer around
at the close of the day
but only to those
who know how to play
and I see you smile
but are you so sure
you can play?

then with fingers of ice
you put out my eyes
and open my side
and tear out my heart
and my lungs, and my spleen
so I can't see you smile
but I see now
how well you play

a maid's lament

you came to me
on a summer's day
you came to me
in sad array
with your battle clothes
your uniform
all torn and deathly grey
I wish I could say more for you
but it's not a happy song

and I took you in
I bathed your wounds
I took your seed
into my womb
lovingly
I tended you
all the summer long
I made you well and whole again
and by winter you were gone

now summer's come again
and your child is born
he looks a lot like you
and his clothes are torn
but one thing
I do swear to you
I will see to as he grows
any maid who may encounter him
will sing a happy song

perfect moment

lips of sunlight
reach in to kiss my soul
oh, perfect moment
such a union to enfold
you glide over me
like a seagull flying
you waken me
your shadow playing
and in return
I offer my morning
hear the gladness
my heart is a ringing bell
taste the water
my love is a brimming well
and it's you who make me full
it's you who kiss my soul

let's paint a picture
where the colours all are sound
let's sing an anthem
that tells of what we found
red for ringing
and green for the morning
grey for your shadow
and gold for love's flowing
and purest whiteness
to halo my saying
for all the world's women
for all of time's applause
for perfect knowledge
for all of nature's laws
I would not trade this love
this chance to learn and give

the swineherd's lament

I'd go to her when the moonlight waned
I'd climb the ivy to her window frame
and she'd reach out, and pull me in
her skin so smooth
and pale and cool
and her eyes so bright
and burning then for me

then one night as the moonlight waned
she appeared downcast in her window frame
and said, 'go now, and don't come again
for you my love
will burn no more
and tonight another man
lies here by me'

and every night when the moonlight waned
I'd stand and stare up through her window frame
and some nights, by her candle flame
I'd see them move
entwined in love
their silhouette
an epitaph for me

then one night as the moonlight waned
the bearded men from the longships came
slew her lover, left her house in flames
and bore my love
away from me
and left me standing
staring out to sea
out to sea
far out to sea

prayer from the trees

I feel you straying my way
soft wind on a stormy day
I hope you know
the way you blow
for only the brave may find me
for I live deep in the trees
and sigh and dream
and dreaming say
if I were a man
I would love you
I've seen men go that way before
it's almost as easy as war

and you who long for me
you must choose what you will be
bright leafy eye
or loving soul
and you must choose all alone
for the woodland tends only its own
but all who choose must know
that those who choose green
may choose never again
unless some redeemer comes
until they are awoken
until they are spoken for

ask and you will receive
seek and you will find
oh, take your time
and then believe
blow and the trees will shed leaves
seek and you will find me
I wait in the branches above you
I have only myself to give you
but release me and I will love you

god's eye

I had no trace of hope
as I lay dying
I could only dimly hear
the vultures crying
I only dimly knew
why they were flying
over me

      and one hundred angels
      then came by
      and they cleared away
      all the dark clouds from the sky
      and they told me that
      the angels' way to die
      may be found by
      those who reach out
      for god's eye
      and enter in

but I just lay
and watched my own blood flow
seep like molten rubies
through the snow
when all at once
a great and golden glow
came from the sky

      and a hundred million angels
      then swept by
      floodlighting the gateway
      to god's eye
      and they bid me bid farewell
      to all goodbyes
      and feel no sorrow
      for tomorrow
      I must follow
      and enter in

then I rose like a phoenix
from the snow
I watched my body bleeding
far below
I was learning all
an angel needs to know
to be reborn

      and all of heaven's angels
      then came by
      and all of heaven trembled
      to their cry
      and they carved a blazing stairway
      to my eye
      and they amazed me
      as I obeyed
      when they bade me
      enter in

the men in the forest

the men in the forest are chopping today
in their doublets and jerkins of leather
the men in the forest are felling their trees
and tying their bodies together

> *and the men in the forest they ask it of me*
> *how foolish can ever a mortal man be?*
> *oh, death and his servants forbid you to know*
> *any tree in the forest could have told you so*

with each new day their clearing grows
as the forest is more thinned
and softer sinks the aspen song
as it shivers in the wind

> *and the men in the forest they ask it of me*
> *how far can the sharpest of mortal eyes see?*
> *they see just as far now as they saw long ago*
> *any tree in the forest could have told you so*

once in their leafy forest roof
the sun peeped through the cracks
but now the roof is falling through
and the sun torments their backs

> *yet the men in the forest they ask it of me*
> *what will shelter us now from the winds off the sea?*
> *let woodland surround you when ocean winds blow*
> *any tree in the forest could have told you so*

the men in the forest are dying today
in their doublets and jerkins of leather
the men in the forest are dying with their trees
and their bodies are falling together

> *but while they still prospered they askèd of me*
> *how many sweet berries grow in the salt sea?*
> *yet the ocean has suffered not one berry to grow*
> *any tree in the forest could have told them so*

a handful of sand

I'm told there's a note on the door
writ bold in your own tiny hand
and the key's in the shed
where we kept it before
covered over with a handful of sand

>I'm sorry, you say
>to have to leave you this way
>I would have told you
>to your face, if you'd been here
>and then there's one or two lines
>about heartache and time
>a bit confused
>although doubtless heartfelt and sincere
>and possibly even quite true

but there's a postscript that says something more
and I must say it sounds a bit lame
it says perfection's a monster
you may crawl towards
but never a soul you can tame

>well it was never my aim
>to conquer and tame
>oh but maybe
>I misunderstand
>for what you mean here to me
>is about as easy to see
>as one lonely grain
>in a handful of sand
>ah, but don't think I'm asking for clues

yes, I'm told there's a note on the door
and I'll read it sometime when I can
then I'll burn it and go for
a stroll on the shore
and choose a new handful of sand

        but I don't mean here
        to mock you or sneer
        indeed there's no way
        I could hold you to blame
        it's just that notes in this vein
        are incurably lame
        your one included
        in fact it sounds much the same
        as the one I was writing to you

lady of the wheels

we're all aboard a train
we're all aboard a train that moves
along golden grooves
in the sky
from which stars are born
as the wheels roll by

> you ask me what it's all about
> well, I'd tell you if I knew
> if I knew what it's all about
> I'd write a song
> and I'd tape the song
> and I'd send that song to you

we're all aboard a train
we're all aboard a train that blows
through her nose
as she wheels through the sky
and the sound of her breathing
is the angels' cry

> still you ask me what it's all about
> again, I'd tell you if I knew
> if I knew what it's all about
> I'd write a song
> and I'd teach you the song
> and I'd sing that song with you

we're all aboard a train
we're all aboard a train whose cars
reach as far
as the ends of the sky
and whose manner of motion
is her own reason why

    once you asked me what it's all about
    I said I'd tell you if I knew
    well, the song is what it's all about
    and you'll find if you do
    as the angels do
    that it's a song you always knew

    and we've all been singing constantly
    and our song will never end
    and no-one needs to write it down
    for the train we're on
    is a cloud of song
    and we're her drops of rain

songs unsung

are those birds that grace the sky
or silver tears within my eyes?
am I really at sea?

is it the sea breeze on my skin
or my own breathing deep within?
that suggests victory?

and how about the drops of spray
or are they only tears of joy
that fall lightly on my tongue?

do harbour sounds excite my ear
or do I dimly begin to hear
the sound of songs unsung?

is this a song of victory?
is it the sea or is it me
that seems to feel so calm?

did I go, or did I stay?
it matters not since either way
I know I'll soon be home

graven faces

ooh, train comes in
change still in the wind
you, you look so fine
and this is how we say goodbye
no game to lose, no need to lie
no shame, no tears, just a gentle kiss
if all the world could be like this

> *but still I find the martyr playing*
> *one more day and the geese go flying*
> *today you hear the statue saying*
> *tomorrow will be long*
> *too long you've been free-wheeling*
> *to ever doubt whoever's dealing*
> *each new card is a woman calling*
> *and you give in*
> *so's not to win*
> *to win would make you proud*

now what of he who plays to win?
who trades his horns and scales for skin?
would you say he's a gambler then?
and will you say he's a gambler still
who burns away his freedom from the wheel? . . .

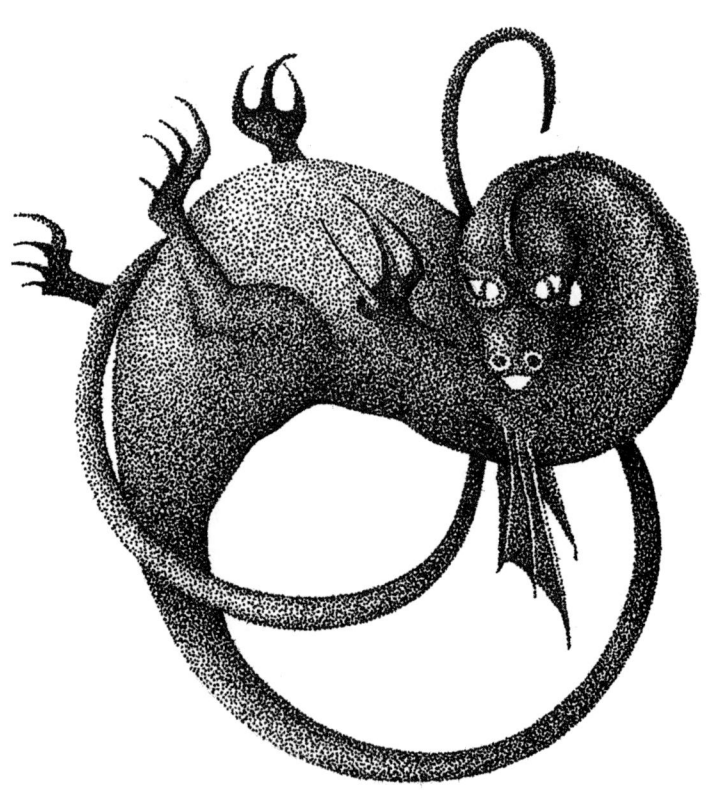

oh, I feel some anger now
take my word and shout it loud
I fear some force will throw the world
like a snowball at a passing galaxy

> *graven faces all so ill*
> *so many empty hours to fill*
> *be sure and act the statue well*
> *it helps to pass the time*
> *if you should miss the time of day*
> *or want some flowers or sympathy*
> *then call me down and ask away*
> *but all that I*
> *can offer you*
> *is the shadow anger leaves*

I've heard and told the ancient tale
where all the graven faces fall
and none remain to wake and wail
but even now I would still believe
the tale that says the circle has no end
and maybe I will
who can tell?
maybe life goes on

still I must be gone

I see your rest has come
full of peaceful dreams
in the morning go find a man
to tell you what they mean

> maybe what I'm doing is wrong
> but still I must be gone
> and I've just got time
> to write these lines
> and leave you with this song

briefly we had fun
playing kings and queens
we thought we were making out
with fine clothes and well-staged scenes

but soon the morning comes
and kills the kings and queens
and this player will be journeying
through the mist and the morning rain

A Song for Atlantis

The offices of the Federated Registry of Unimpeachable Music Publishers were situated on the tenth floor of a twelve-storey building in the West End. When Jane was ushered into the large, plush-carpeted, generously windowed boardroom she found only one other person present.

This was the Philosopher.

He was tall, thin, stooped, in his middle thirties, and frowning gloomily while listening to a Walkman cassette player. Jane walked round the varnished pine table. On it were eight stapled sheaves of lyrics, spaced like placemats for dinner, and two plates of biscuits. She sat two places distant from the frowning Philosopher and quietly inspected the topmost lyric in front of her. It began:

> I LOVE YOU
> I LOVE YOU
> BABY I LOVE YOU SO
> I LOVE YOU
> I LOVE YOU
> BABY PLEASE DON'T GO
> I LOVE YOU . . .

'Pathetic,' muttered the Philosopher.

'Yes,' Jane agreed, off guard. 'I'm sorry,' she recovered quickly. 'What is pathetic?'

The Philosopher introduced himself unenthusiastically and explained that he had been listening to a demonstration recording of two songs received in the post that morning from an aspiring songwriter. 'Read that,' he said uninvitingly, scrutinizing Jane's trim figure and neat appearance while passing her a flimsy scrap of paper which said:

'Dear Mr Philosopher, please find the cassette of my two latest songs which I am enclosing. It is now a year since I last had the pleasure of sending you my compositions. Lately Ive been having to neglect my songwriting sadly. This is due to lack of funds and also endevering not to get thrown off my Anthropology Deggree.

Otherwise my drummer has left me and reverted to his Guiness. However I do feel strongly that my song writing has strengthened imeasurably. The first song entitled *Bloodlit Nites* is all about being raped by a randy lady Vampire. I do hope you will appreciate the satirical twist. I dont suppose Cliff Richard will want to sing it, but can you please get it to his attention? If so I will be happy to forgo my normal statutry advance of seven hundred . . . '

'Bloody vampires,' the Philosopher commented. 'Why always vampires?'

'Aren't his songs good, then?' asked Jane, returning the letter.

'Actually they could be worse. The recordings are diabolical, but the songs are less unoriginal than ninety per cent of what we'll hear this afternoon.'

'Oh,' said Jane. 'I thought we were selecting from the best fifty entries.'

'The *final* fifty entries.'

'What's the difference?' Jane asked innocently.

'The *best* entries have already been eliminated.'

'Surely not,' said Jane. 'Surely . . . '

'You haven't previously undergone the pleasure of Atlantovision judging, have you?' the Philosopher speculated.

'No.'

'And what were your boss's instructions?'

'Um . . . ' Jane blushed and reached for a digestive biscuit to cover her embarrassment.

'Exactly. I'll tell you, shall I? "We can't vote for our own songs," he said. "It's against the rules. So if you hear anything good, give it *bottom* marks. Everything else give *low* marks, and that way our songs might scrape through with *mediocre* marks. Got it?"'

This was so verbatim what Jane's boss had told her that she felt obliged to change the subject. 'Don't you like being a music publisher?' she asked with forced interest.

'No.'

'Why do you do it?'

'I can't do anything else. My brain cells have gone the way of all strong ale.'

'But, I mean, not to be rude, of course, but you don't quite . . . look . . . '

The Philosopher sighed and raked some lank white fingers through his greasy brown hair. Again looking wistfully at Jane's pleasant but unremarkable physique, he said:

'Evolution has got the better of me. Like sharks and merchant bankers, I took a wrong turning at a crucial stage. For a while at university my partner and I were going to become a sort of upmarket Rolling Stones. But gradually we didn't. So now we feed the wolf with jingles for commercial radio. "Things go better with sugar, salt and cholesterol." That's my line.'

Jane thought this rather pitiful, but before she could muster a sympathetic remark the door burst open and the other members of the Listening Panel arrived very loudly.

Five minutes later they were ready to begin.

At the head of the table sat the Chairperson, a small fat wheezy man in his fifties. At one o'clock from the Chairperson was the Joker, a Northern character in a suit of denims that might once have been stylish. Next, the Stunner, a model beauty with natural blonde hair, flawless blue eyes, a captivating smile, a laugh seductive as the breeze caressing the sundrenched uppermost leaves of a tropical rainforest, and nothing to say.

On the Stunner's left was the Superstar, a million-selling songwriter in a tight cream-coloured cashmere sweater and several gold bracelets. Self-consciously slumming, he lit an Emperor-size cigarette immediately and spoke only by way of condescending reply to ingratiating questions from the Whizkid.

The Whizkid sat at the Mummy end of the table, facing the Chairperson. Still in his early twenties, he wore a stylish three-piece striped suit, a prominent Rolex watch, and was obviously becoming Big in the Business by dint of fawning diligence combined with two dwarvish, lobeless, equally tone-deaf ears. At seven o'clock from the Whizkid was Jane, and between Jane and the Philosopher towered the Behemoth. This was a formidable personage with long peroxide-streaked rat-tails, spectacles thick as binoculars, more necklaces than Jane could politely distinguish, a bosom like Vesuvius, and a bellicose baritone voice achieved jointly by nature and the chainsmoking of filter-tipped cheroots.

Behind the Whizkid was a powerful hifi system operated by a scrawny youth with waist-length hair, whom FRUMP had borrowed from the nearest Unemployment Centre for the afternoon.

'Roll it, please, Daniel,' the Chairperson wheezed.

Daniel inserted the first cassette, the Chairperson started a large stopwatch, and the boardroom was deafened by the incessant repetition of:

> I LOVE YOU
> I LOVE YOU
> BABY I LOVE YOU SO
> I LOVE YOU . . .

Suddenly Jane realized with a spasm of gratitude that the torture had paused. The Chairperson had raised a runt sausage of a forefinger, and Daniel had stopped the cassette.

'Just goes to show, doesn't it,' drawled the Joker, 'how long two minutes can be?'

'Do we really only listen to two minutes of each song?' asked Jane, who thought this rather unfair.

'Put it this way, sweetheart,' said the Joker patronizingly, 'would *you* want to listen to that for a second longer than you had to?'

'Watch it, you,' rumbled the Behemoth. 'How do you know that isn't *my* song?'

'Would you confess if it were?' inquired the Philosopher.

The Behemoth looked severely at the Philosopher and snarled: 'Are *you* Jewish?'

'Not physically, but . . . '

'Next, please, Daniel.'

Jane's ears were still so numb from the first song that she forgot to turn to the second lyric, but her impression was of a two-minute one-note repetition of:

> YEW ANCHORS CAN OILS ODD OFF

'Liquid engineering,' cackled the Joker.

'Are we allowed to give zero marks?' Jane asked seriously.

'I'm afraid not, my dear,' the Chairperson regretted understandingly. 'The songs are all anonymous, to ensure impartiality, and the rules require us to give each title a mark from one to six.'

'Because', added the Joker, 'if we could give *no* marks, we might end up with *all* the numbers getting none, and then have to hear them all *again*.'

The Philosopher groaned faintly.

Jane looked disapprovingly at her marksheet and gave *Yew Anchors* one mark. The corner of her left eye was surprised to see that the Behemoth gave it three.

Coffee was brought in by the FRUMP secretary and the Chairperson hurriedly excused himself.

'Not a bad little sod,' said the Behemoth. 'Plumbing isn't too watertight, but his heart's in the right place.'

'And full of cholesterol,' said the Philosopher.

'Know why he's Chairperson?' the Joker asked Jane.

'No. Why?'

'His poor old brain's so boozed away he never remembers to get bored.'

Jane took refuge in scanning the lyric for the next song.

The Chairperson returned, beaming sheepishly, dunked a caramel wafer in his sweet creamy coffee, and signalled for the torture to continue. This it did with a slow, tedious, predictable ballad, crooned with infinite false emotion by a gutless tenor.

'Now there's a classy ballad,' murmured the Joker, whose company published it.

'But not a monster,' objected the Whizkid, whose company did not.

'Instantly memorable melody,' purred the Joker.

'But lacking killer hooks,' insisted the Whizkid.

'What is a monster with killer hooks?' asked Jane, whose mind was full of images from *Peter Pan*.

'Ask him,' said the Philosopher, nodding spitefully at the Superstar. 'He writes two each morning before breakfast.'

The Superstar nodded complacently and lit another cigarette. Of these he consumed four per hour, with clockwork regularity, and had done since his teens, when he read in an early Saint story that the miraculous Templar's practice was to smoke just so.

Large and bony was the Superstar's head, cropped and colourless his hair, and his nose? Like a crushed Dutch carrot, Jane felt. Even if he was a millionaire, she could barely imagine herself ever . . .

'Next, please, Daniel,' the Chairperson spluttered breathlessly.

The boardroom was by now pleasantly bronchial with carcinogens from the Superstar's cigarettes and the Behemoth's cheroots. Late November sunshine shone flatly through the generous FRUMP windows, gently shimmered by an uplifting current of leaded filth from the crawling city streets below.

Jane blew her nose delicately and listened to a comparably haunting refrain entitled:

BY WHICH I MEAN . . .

'Pass the dictionary,' said the Joker to the Stunner, when the Chairperson lifted his guillotine finger.

The Stunner's breathtaking bijou beauty rewarded the Joker's slavering with a luxurious silky laugh.

'Neil Sedaka does not sing "by which",' nodded the Behemoth.

'Whatever happened to lyric writers: that's what I'd like to know?' said the Whizkid confidently.

The Superstar nodded sapiently, and the Philosopher passed Jane a note behind the Behemoth's bulbous back. Jane unfolded the note discreetly and read:

'*See what I mean? That incomparably haunting refrain was in fact written by **myself**. It's one of my finest songs. These people are **philistines**.*'

Jane acknowledged the Philosopher's communication with a noncommittal encouraging smile. Then her attention was violently rocked by:

LOVE BABY LOVE BABY LOVE, OH OH OH
LOVE BABY LOVE BABY LOVE, OH OH OOOH . . .

The lead vocal on this noisome entertainment was delivered as by a six-year-old schoolboy with laryngitis. Jane felt herself swelling with righteous anger.

> LOVE BABY LOVE BABY LOVE BABY LOVE!
> OOOOOOH . . .

'Enough!' croaked the Chairperson, for the hirsute Daniel had not noticed his guillotine finger, being far away in a colourful men's lifestyle magazine.

'Well, really,' cried Jane indignantly. 'That really is *pathetic*. Isn't it? It's a blatant imitation of *Baby Love Baby*, and – ' here Jane received from the Behemoth a poke in the ribs that would leave her bruised for weeks, but too late to prevent her finishing:

'Even *I* could sing better than that. And that really is saying something.'

It wasn't the pregnant silence itself that told her she had boobed. More the realization that the Joker had failed to quip. The Stunner was blushing demurely into the rhapsodic blue froth of the Swiss voile dress embracing her peerless high cleavage. The Philosopher's envious eyes were pelting the Stunner with an agonizing volley of rampant lust, weary self-loathing, aloof revulsion, and impossible undying devotion.

Only now did Jane perceive the horrific oneness of the Stunner and the feeble laryngitic performer of *Love Baby Love*. 'Oh,' she gasped, appalled. 'I didn't . . . I'm sorry, I . . . '

The Behemoth chuckled dirtily:

'Never mind, deary. You'll learn.'

'I hope not,' said the Philosopher, and the afternoon concluded without further incident.

The following week the telephone rang while Jane was drying her hair. It was the Philosopher.

'Will you have dinner with me?' he asked bluntly.

'That's very kind of you,' stammered Jane. 'But . . . '

'What?'

'Why me? Frankly. Why not the Stunner? You see, I couldn't help noticing the way you were looking at her the other day. Wouldn't you rather take her to dinner?'

'Yes.'

'Oh.'

'Just as I'd rather have a Botticelli original on my living-room wall than a humble Victorian water-colour.'

Thanks very much, thought Jane with heat.

'But then what would happen?'

'What would then happen?' Jane asked shortly.

'Either I couldn't afford the instalments on my Botticelli, or I couldn't afford to insure her adequately. Anyway she would soon be stolen from me, and from the very pinnacle of bliss I should inevitably plummet to the deepest pit of the blackest despair. And so, being a realistic pessimist, I ask you instead:

'Please have dinner with me tomorrow? I'm not at all romantic or rich. I'm neither frightfully handsome nor pre-eminently penial. But I do have a modest way with words, don't I? I'm not unreasonably inconsiderate, and I'm fifteen times more forthright than anyone else in FRUMP. I admire your body. I'm sure in time I could relish your other attributes equally. So you will have dinner with me, won't you? Please?'

'No,' said Jane. She liked to think she wasn't unduly emotionally demanding, or sexually voracious, but she did have higher hopes than this. 'I'm sorry. I'm afraid I can't. But thank you for thinking of me.'

'Just as I thought. But not to worry. Well, goodbye.'

'Goodbye.'

Three months later Jane was bumped into by the Behemoth in a West End boutique. Jane was looking for the right colour of tights, and the Behemoth was vigorously trying on a satin trousersuit that made her look like a gold-lamé Michelin Man in high-heeled green boots. Had Jane heard the latest FRUMP tattle?

No. What was it?

Well! The Superstar, under various pseudonyms and through divers publishing companies, had written seven of the eight finalists in the SONG FOR ATLANTIS contest. These included *I Love You* and *Love Baby Love*, but not *Yew Anchors*, which was very much an outsider according to the bookmakers. The Whizkid had left EBK to manage the Superstar's escalating fleet of companies. The Joker's company had gone bankrupt, and The Joker was now driving a wine merchant's delivery van. And!

Yes?

The Chairperson had died of a heart attack, and the Philosopher was in hospital.

How terrible. Why?

Savagely beaten up by a band of unemployed teenage songwriters who had not valued his free advice concerning their abilities and aspirations.

'Longwinded arsehole,' said the Behemoth jovially. 'Serves him right.'

Jane could not agree. She felt remorseful. As if the Philosopher's injuries were somehow *her* fault. When she visited he was in a room of his own, to prevent his pessimism infecting the other patients. She had brought him some mixed nuts and raisins, but he couldn't eat them as his head was still in a plastercast like a spaceman's helmet. His right leg was in traction and he was very weak, but still able to speak.

Jane tried to cheer him up by telling him about her new job. She had recently been appointed personal assistant to the Musical Director of the Albion Broadcasting Company, and in three weeks she would be accompanying him to the final of the ATLANTOVISION SONG CONTEST itself, in Memphis.

'Did you secure this magnificent post through the agency that got successful by bothering people for more money?' the Philosopher whispered sourly.

'You mustn't be so cynical,' said Jane, laughing, warming to his helpless inadequacy. 'It doesn't suit you.'

'Yes it does,' he sighed. 'That's the trouble. It suits me right down to my splintered ankle.'

At this point the hospital radio broadcast *Love Baby Love*, written by the Superstar and performed by the Stunner and the Stunnettes. This song had won the national SONG FOR ATLANTIS competition the previous week (despite twenty-five sarcastic comments by Ersish Shamrock Hogan, the ubiquitous ABC compere, and hence would be representing Albion in Memphis.

'And here's a juicy newsflash for all you patient people,' trilled the hospital disc jockey when the song was over. 'At a champagne reception in the West End this morning the Superstar and the Stunner made public, yes, break your hearts now, their intention to wed the afternoon following ATLANTOVISION. Isn't that *fantastic?*'

The Philosopher shuddered. His one visible eyelid fluttered shut.

In Memphis Jane found the ATLANTOVISION occasion extravagant, spectacular, grandiose, and interminably depressing. Was this due to the host nation's insistence on repeating all information in seventeen languages? *Love Baby Love* took an early lead but was soon overtaken by the Mesopotamia entry, whose chorus proclaimed:

> MESOPOTAMIA, SUNNY AND HOT
> MESOPOTAMIA'S GOT THE LOT
> MESOPOTAMIA'S NOT, NOT, NOT
> A COLD AND RAINY SORT OF SPOT
> OT, OT
> OT, OT
> NO, MESOPOTAMIA'S GOT THE LOT!

For three hours Mesopotamia kept a comfortable nose in front and millions of people all over Atlantis fell asleep in their armchairs or went out for a drink. 'You should probably just have time for a couple of dozen quick ones before we get through all this lot,' as Shamrock Hogan put it in tones of weary disgust on the Albion television soundtrack.

But then *Love Baby Love* was jerked back into the running by Xanadu, who bore a traditional grudge against Mesopotamia on account of racist atrocities committed over millenia past. The Xanadu jury gave *Love Baby Love* twelve points and Mesopotamia only one. From here it was a neck-and-neck two-cart-horse race until everything hinged on the final set of marks from the Zoilean Free State.

Jane sensed that her boss, the ABC Musical Director, was becoming intensely nervous. He was a strongly-built man in his late forties, with male-pattern baldness, gold-rimmed spectacles, and a pugnacious chin. Just before the Zoilean marks came in Jane glimpsed the Musical Director chewing his knuckles and sweating over his tuxedo like a lemon-squeezer overflowing.

Then the television fastened like an electronic leech on a close-up of the Stunner weeping hysterically in the Superstar's white velvet arms as it was announced that the Zoilean jury had exercised its small-print right to award *Love Baby Love* zero marks in view of the bare-faced plagiarisms involved.

'How can four notes and three words be plagiarized, Lord save us?' As Shamrock Hogan put it with such eloquent poignancy.

In any case Mesopotamia had won this year's ATLANTOVISION CONTEST and millions of people all over Atlantis switched off their televisions before the winning entry could be repeated.

'Thank God for that,' muttered the Musical Director, mopping his streaming neck.

'What do you mean?' asked Jane. 'You sound *pleased*.'

'Of course I'm pleased, you silly girl.'

'But *why?*' insisted Jane, bewildered.

'Because if we'd won,' the Musical Director explained with ponderous patience, 'we'd have had to host the whole bloody thing ourselves, in Albion, next year.'

'But surely that's part of the honour and privilege of winning, isn't it?'

'Certainly not. It's a farce. It costs a fortune to produce, and we can't afford it. The Government doesn't give us enough money. Nobody watches it except between the advertisements on the commercial channel, and, besides, it would have meant an enormous amount of *extra work for me*.'

'I see,' said Jane.

The following week she visited the Philosopher again. It was a sunny May day, so she took a bunch of brilliant parrot tulips to banish his bedside gloom. He was hobbling about on crutches now, had shed his spacehelmet, and was pleased to see her – so far as she could tell. He had seen ATLANTOVISION on ABC television, but when Jane related to him, with resilient disapproval, the Musical Director's confidential remarks, the Philosopher immediately moaned pathetically and begged Jane to marry him as soon as possible.

'I need your commonsense cheerfulness,' he urged her desperately, 'to cushion me against the infernal jagged *futility* of The Whole Sordid Business.'

Jane gave him a long, hard, but not unloving look.

'No,' she said regretfully. 'I'm afraid I can't. But thank you for thinking of me.'

Part III

LATER 1970s

the brightest smile

I was a lonely pilgrim
knocking at life's front door
till you bathed me
in more harmony
than I'd ever known before

> down the longest mile
> in the weirdest style
> keep on smiling the brightest smile
> oh, sweet moonchild
> in the sweet meanwhile
> no-one can argue with the brightest smile

you teased away my sorrow
you showed me the angels' way
now my time wings free
as a wild honeybee
through the flowers of the wide long day

and I will build a castle
on the hill where the angels play
with a treasury
full of harmony
and I'll take you there some day

drowning

here we are drowning within sight of land
all because no one will take command
mermaids are sighing and shaking their heads
and holding their tongues
but you know what they'll say when we're dead?

    they'll say we could have had good times
    we could have had good days
    we could have had good nights as well

so much worry and trouble and fret
here we are drowning and worrying yet
Neptune is sighing and loading his gun
and saying we would have lived longer
if only we could have had fun

well suppose there's a god and a heaven above
and life everlasting and infinite love
then we'll sing joyous praises and swear to be good
and all heaven's angels will tell us
we should have had fun while we could

real hard case

little lady, friend of mine
I think about you all the time
and just to prove you're on my mind
I'm singing you this song

> I'm trying as never before to give
> I'd like to give you all I have
> I never believed I could fall in love
> but it seems that I was wrong

if I tell you I'm a real hard case
and without you I would wither and waste
and there's no-one else can take your place
will you realize how I feel?

> or will you tell me I'm trying too hard
> like a teenage Dylan in a coffee bar
> or poor old Einstein trying to harness the stars
> and himself in a unified field?

little lady, here's looking at you
I know I'm not saying anything new
the difference is I'm saying it to you
and I really mean what I say

> I go walking by the cemetery
> where the dead men cry out for company
> and I promise I will join them instantly
> if you should go your way

but see I'm saying it all with a smile
only so can you make the world worthwhile
I'd rather lose you than to spoil your style
as I'm sure someday you will see

the emperor and the geisha girl

born in the germ of the story
the emperor hears of satori
the geisha girl revels in rumours
the emperor loves a good drama

      on the cape of their play pen
      they stage an all-night let's-pretend

they hear the curtain-call calling
the geisha girl acts as the fräulein
playing a part fit to pursue her
the emperor choses the führer

      eagles, cross and a goosestep too
      no typecast could be more true

the geisha girl's cheeks are too rosy
she renders the emperor uneasy
he thinks she thinks he's a fairy
so how will he conquer satori?

      champagne sheets and a witches brew
      a shaft, a sword and a dildo too

the geisha girl wears a blue toga
sleeps in the emperor's pagoda
the emperor wears the pagoda
sleeps in the wings of the saga

      morning opens but two eyes
      no more rosy cheeks will rise . . .

the geisha girl lies bleeding
the emperor goes into hiding
says he has conquered satori
but everyone knows he's a fairy

      stows his guilt in sanctuary
      strange that it should trouble me

now everything seems to be swaying
pagodas seem to be flying
how can I tell if I'm moving?
assurance now would be soothing

crazy delight

crazy delight
there's a party tonight
there's a bowl of white light
and red wine
there's a great blonde woman
in a wisp of lace
aiming herself at me
and I want nothing
but to see your face
and I know that may not be

> but oh, my lover
> I will love no other
> though blood may rain from the sky
> I will take lovers
> but I'll love no other
> since something inside me died
> when you lied
> and you didn't even say goodbye

crazy delight
oh, crazy delight
what a crazy delight
we take in causing pain
there's a great blonde woman
in a wisp of lace
wants to hear me talk about you
and I want nothing
but to leave this place
yet there's no place I want to go to

weed's warning

rising high?
well so can I
careful I don't pass you by
flesh and bone
humble homes
buildings easily overgrown

> hey, you'd better believe me
> I'm green, but I'm not easy
> I die, but I grow again

cut me down
burn the ground
help yourselves, build your town
put up your towers
but I'm no flower
some day soon you may feel my power

trees, my old companions
share my opinions
earth, our holy mother
taught us to love each other

we don't hate
nor does fate
we only claim our own estate
so fare you well
build and swell
who will prosper? time will tell

sober serious man

I was a sober serious man
with serious work to do
tending the flames of the stolen fire
until I met you
now here I sit smoking my lungs away
and drinking the whole night through
letting my brain go down the drain
and all on account of you
but you don't care

and I knew it from the start
I knew you'd break my heart
when first I clapped my eyes
upon your neon-sign-like smile
and I knew I'd be tongue-tied
unable to decide
whether I should take the plunge
and bare to you my soul
or sit tight and hold my tongue
as I have always done
wherever I thought there was half a chance
that I might lose my freedom
to think and talk and sing
and come and go as I please
so here am I now torn again
between the devil and the deep blue sea
and neither one cares

I see you going with another man
without qualities
and I think if you can sink to him
you may as well sink to me
yes, you might as well go all the way
you're already breaking the rule
that the prettiest women give themselves away
to money fast cars and fools
or devil-may-care

*don't you know
I'm in love
with you?*
but I dare say you won't know
no, I dare say it won't show
I'm never one to spread it round
or wear it on my face
whenever I'm in love
and I don't know what to do
I just sing to myself by candlelight
or in the early morning dew
where no-one cares

now I've sung my song and done my best
to make a slave of you
and each in its own peculiar way
not a word is untrue
thus I love you most of all the things
that live beneath the sun
and yet I have to hope you've guessed
that when all is said and done
and underneath the agony
I say it all in fun
and I don't really care

soapsuds in my gravy

times are coming on hard in
an octopus's garden
I can't help feeling something's wrong

> and yet I'm so far below
> I don't know
> what's going on
> pa, pa, pa . . .

soapsuds in my gravy
poison from the navy
somebody must be crazy

my tentacles are shrinking
I wish I was better at thinking
there must be something I could do

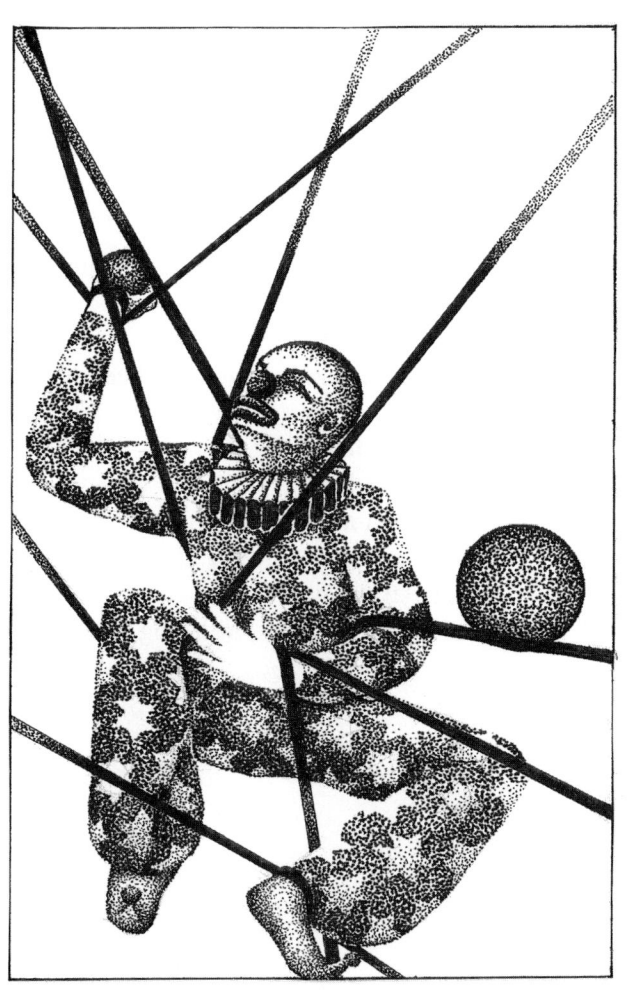

the very first song

the very first song
that ever I sang
I sang to young love waking
to young love's pains
and long lonely hours
and young love's first forsaking

I sang from my heart
though I sang scarcely well
I sang a song of my own making
I sang to my love
and oft-times to myself
I sang to ease my aching

I sang a tale of joy
and a tale of woe
I sang a hymn to sweet-sad feelings
I sang in praise
of all that was
and my wounds have long been healing

the very first song
that ever I sang
has been a long time dying
but I could not sing it
honestly now
and I see no sense in trying

from the heart

pains and presidents come and go
so do singers, sand and snow
the singer fades, the song remains
then has the singer sung in vain?
the world's a play, so we're sometimes told
and I believe it now I'm growing old

> right now I am singing from the heart
> but how long can I play this part?

kings and pawns and serving girls
make their moves across the world
some go carefree, some forlorn
either way it's the way they're born
me, I have no cross to bear
I just sing my song for all to share

I feel my body breaking down
soon be going beneath the ground
worms and fishes, play my tune
I'll be on your menu soon
losers only can complain
it's just what we pay for what we gain

sitting there

I was sitting in the station café
waiting for my train
drinking British Rail black coffee
and getting heartburn for my pains
when this woman came to me pointing
I thought she wanted my chocolate éclair
but she was pointing at the chair beside me
and saying: is anybody sitting there?

> sitting there?
> sitting there?
> is anybody sitting there?

I boarded my train really early
and I was planning on a peaceful read
so I got myself a compartment
in accordance with my needs
when in burst this crowd of schoolgirls
all legs and breasts and hair
I thought they wanted my body
but they just said: is anybody sitting there?

well if I get up to heaven
find myself all alone
with nowhere left to go to
except a staircase leading to a throne
then I will breathe in deeply
brush my wings and comb my hair
and I will mount that staircase
and say: is anybody sitting there?

McCandy's chorus

I want my tomorrow now
women, wealth and fame and power
I never thought I'd see this hour
but I want my tomorrow now

>I want it now
>and I want it bad
>all life's joys
>I never had
>I want my tomorrow now
>don't want to beg and borrow
>just want my tomorrow
>I want my tomorrow *now*

and I only want what's due to me
I'm not asking for immortality
so you people had better believe
I want my tomorrow now

on my way

oh, pretty lady
I don't mean to be unkind
but I'm tired of being lazy
and I'm leaving you behind

so let's have no tears
you'd be wasting your time
I've been here a year
and I've made up my mind
I'm on my way

> hear my goodbye
> for the wind's got my eye
> I'm on my way

clouds race by above me
chase wild geese to the west
sweet-soft winds do love me
going to blow till I come to rest

I see your tears
but you're wasting your time
I've been here a year
and I've made up my mind
I'm on my way

I don't know where I'm going
but I'll write when I get there
and if you still want to be with me
I'll try and send you the fare

so you might as well smile
else you'll be wasting your time
it's the end of the year
and I've made up my mind
I'm on my way

a memory framed for ever

the early morning sun invades your doorway
like an early morning rose you catch my sleeve
and shed a morning tear that makes me tremble
for you must stay, I know, and I must leave

I leave you with a gift most freely given
I leave you with a love no hate can kill
I leave you with a memory framed for ever
and I leave you with a space no-one can fill

no need for you to ask me why I'm leaving
no need for me to ask why you must stay
our choices all are made while we lie sleeping
the choice lives on, and the reasons fade away

now the early morning sun brings you a shadow
as to me an early morning kiss you blow
and I see now I'm bound to leave you smiling
I think early morning is the only time it could be so

looking forward to summer

it's April
and there's warmth in the breeze
there's new life
in the fields and the trees
and I want you for my lover
but I can't wait for ever
though that seems to be what you want

> yes, I'm looking forward to summer
> all I need is a lover
> take me or I'll find another
> though it's you I really want

take me
and we'll join the bees
we'll make honey
with great pleasure and ease
we'll go walking together
we'll take a boat on the river
and feed the baby swans

the eye

out there over the ocean
a storm is gathering
the waves are curling angrily
and the gulls are sheltering
and the trawlermen take to the taverns again
retelling tales of old times
and the tallest tale
that takes most ale
is the one about me and my crime
I don't deny my shame

>   but oh, what I'd give
>   if I only could live
>   my whole life over again
>   I'd live it differently

I was born an omen
the eye of a hurricane
my voice roared out destruction
and my blood poured down like rain
and swept the fields and the houses away
and washed the light from the sky
and the more I roared
the more it poured
till my heart was all run dry
and I lay down to die

a sailor's plight

come all you pretty maidens
if you have no man tonight
gather yourselves around me
and I'll tell you of my plight

> for I'm alone
> just a lonely sailor boy
> with just my song to give
> I'm alone
> just a lonely sailor boy
> and I need a woman's love

once I had a sweetheart
and together we did lie
my head pillowed on her breast
her hand upon my thigh
but she was taken from me
whereof I care not why
just hope to find another
sometime before I die

so come all you pretty maidens
if you have no man tonight
there is surely one among you
who would ease a sailor's plight

take me away

sometimes I'd like to move among the stars
sometimes I'd like to be where film stars are
and at times like this I'd like someone
to take me far away
somewhere to wander
and somewhere to stay

> take me away
> take me to Hollywood
> or along the milky way
> take me where there's someone
> who can hear what I say

take me to heaven for a day
or where the deer and the antelope play
take me where you will
oh, but take me out of here
the ceiling is too low
and the walls are too near

> take me away
> take me to Hollywood
> or heaven for a day
> and I'll still be asking you
> to take me away

rainy eye

there's a cloud like a knife in the sky
and it looks like there's rain in your eye
there's a sighing in the wind
and it sounds like goodbye
I'm sorry I can't give you more

>   I'm sorry I can't give you more
>   sorry I can't give you more
>   rainy eye
>   goodbye, goodbye
>   I'm sorry I can't give you more

don't tell me, I know how it feels
your whole world an old battlefield
last night I was your sword
but I can't be your shield
and I'm sorry I can't give you more

and it's not between right and wrong
it's just that I don't belong
I gave you some love
and I give you my song
and I'm sorry I can't give you more

moonlight shines

I go walking
by the river
hope to see you there
don't know why
I got no reason
I know you won't be there
but I'm in love with you

>and moonlight shines
>on mysteries
>moonlight shines on clues
>moonlight shines on me tonight
>may moonlight shine on you

moonlight shines
upon the water
swans go floating by
stormy king
with smoky children
and his snow-white bride
reminding me of you

oh, pretty baby
I bet you're sleeping
would that I knew where
I'd buy wings
and fly beside you
take you to my lair
and make a queen of you

close your eyes

hush and be still, you have nothing to fear
it's only the wind in the willows you hear
and what could go wrong with your lover so near?

> close your eyes
> the hours are flickering by
> close your eyes
> I'll sing you a lullaby
> close your eyes
> bid care goodbye
> and I'll sing you to sleep

there's a sweet smell of cider from the farm
and the moon hanging huge like a golden charm
and you could never be further from harm

the swallows are leaving

I see a dark hollow where we lay side by side
I see on my pillow that someone has cried
and I see from your letter that someone has lied
in a tissue of intricate weaving
and I see in the mirror that something has died
and I see the swallows are leaving

> I see gold
> and silver and blue
> and the first white of cold
> where the frost hits the dew
> I see a faint shadow
> where once I saw you
> and I see the swallows are leaving

I see why you left me, but not why you cried
I see why you wrote me, but not why you lied
I see you've decided what you had to decide
and though I'm no great one for grieving
I see a great emptiness, mouth gaping wide
and I see the swallows are leaving

The Philosopher's Mother

In 1788, in Danzig, a famous child was born.

Its mother, Johanna Schopenhauer, had light brown hair, clear blue eyes, and dainty proportions. Later she would become a celebrated novelist. Today, at twenty-two, she was two decades younger than her husband. When, during the afternoon, Heinrich Schopenhauer entered his counting-house he announced:

'A son.'

Exploiting his employer's deafness, a humorous book-keeper exclaimed:

'If he's like his papa, he *will* be a pretty baboon!'

Johanna disagreed. 'I was *sure*,' she said, 'there was never a handsomer child than my Arthur.'

Their home was a beautiful villa in a large garden surrounded by box trees, with a sloping view of woods and fields, and the ship-dotted Baltic beyond.

But the French Revolution had begun in 1789. Europe was in uproar, and Danzig was blockaded in 1793. 'My husband and I', wrote Johanna, 'resolved, at great sacrifice, to quit our native city.' So the five-year-old Arthur was whisked from Danzig to Hamburg, which retained its liberty.

The Schopenhauers shared a wanderlust, and when Arthur was fifteen his parents took him on a two-year tour of Europe. While Heinrich and Johanna explored Scotland, Arthur was left at a school in Wimbledon. There he mastered English so well that even Londoners took him to be English.

On their return to Hamburg, Arthur had promised his father, he would begin a business apprenticeship. Here he became deeply depressed, seeing before him nothing but dusty ledgers and boring arithmetic.

A few months later Heinrich died, falling from a warehouse window into the canal below, and rumour spread of suicide. Arthur's grief for his father was profound. He also felt his only hope of freedom was lost – like a precious key dropped overboard. For who now could undo his promise to enter business?

Meanwhile, Johanna removed her widowhood, and her daughter, to Weimar – hoping for livelier companions than the respectable Hamburgers. Two weeks after her arrival, the bloody battle of Jena was fought nearby, and Napoleon defeated the Prussians.

In October 1806 Johanna wrote:

'The cannons roared again. Awfully near. Oh, my Arthur! The bare recollection makes me tremble. Now the cannons thundered, the floor shook, and the windows rattled. How near death was!'

Of the aftermath:

'The hospital dead are now carried away, and no longer lie in heaps on the streets. No-one, my son, can know the horrors of war, unless he sees them close. I know how misery grieves you, my Arthur, but as yet you know nothing of it.'

Back in Hamburg the young philosopher was jotting his thoughts under cover of ledgers, and playing truant from his office – to attend university lectures.

Johanna was horrified. But she loved her Arthur dearly, and when she realized how miserable he was, she consulted her Weimar friends:

'Is it too late for him to change careers?'

'Late,' the learned gentlemen agreed, 'but not too late.'

Arthur greeted his liberation with a flood of joyful tears, then hastened to the Gymnasium in Gotha. There he took private lessons in Latin and Greek, and made astonishing progress in all subjects – revelling in knowledge like a dolphin restored to the sea.

He also went through a worldly phase: keeping company with aristocrats, following fashion, and courting pretty ladies. Soon he was spending so much, on clothes and entertainments, that even the easy-going Johanna had to urge:

'*Economy*, darling!'

'Seldom, mother,' retorted Arthur, 'has a sooty kettle been accused by a blacker pot.'

Displeased by such sarcasms, Johanna arranged for Arthur to study in lodgings on the far side of town.

'It is needful to my happiness,' she said, 'to know that you are happy. But not that I witness the fact. Your ill-humour, complaints, sullen looks, the extraordinary opinions you utter, like oracles no-one may contradict; all this depresses me, without helping you.'

For peace to complete his doctorate, Arthur fled to a little town in the forest, thirty miles from Weimar. And in November 1813 Dr Schopenhauer, aged twenty-five, returned to Weimar, to find his mother a best-selling celebrity.

According to Adele:

'Our mother enjoyed the society of the most distinguished men. She pleased and made herself beloved. Her conversational powers made her house the centre of intellectual life.'

Not everyone was so kind. One of Johanna's visitors, a lawyer, recorded in his diary:

'Madame Schopenhauer. Rich widow. Professes erudition. Authoress. Prattles much. Eager for applause. Constantly smiling to herself. God preserve us from such women.'

This was closer to Arthur's view. His waspish pessimism and his mother's butterfly optimism increasingly clashed. When he proudly presented her with his first book, she exclaimed:

'*The Fourfold Root*! A treatise for apothecaries?'

'It will be read, mother,' snorted Arthur, 'when no drawing-room will contain a single copy of your novels.'

Johanna smiled knowingly.

'Your entire edition,' she prophesied, 'will rot in the publisher's warehouse.'

Both predictions proved veridical. Though Arthur's philosophy has survived, most of his first edition became waste paper. Meanwhile his mother's novels were devoured, and for years the prickly thinker would bristle like a furious porcupine at the admiring question:

'Are *you* the son of the famous Johanna Schopenhauer?'

Part IV

EARLIER 1980s

here I am

once I did believe
in perfect truth and love
and I saved myself
like an old man's wealth
for a girl that the world
never has seen nor will see

> but now I just say
> hey, here I am
> you be my woman
> and I'll be your man

it's just like writing a song
you can write it proud and strong
and well conceal
what you really feel
or you can tell it all
in a short word or two

and so we are alone
the restful souls have flown
you and I
are left with the night
and we can either grow together
or wither alone

beautiful pirate

if I'd known we would only be ships in the night
I would have passed you by, by the pale moonlight
and set sail
for a coral reef in the south seas
for the whales
the lotus girls and the palm trees

>sail with me
>you said sweetly
>but then you burned my sails
>why did you burn my sails?

like a beautiful pirate you came aboard
and I gave you more treasure than I could afford
and by dawn
my rigging was hanging in flames
you were gone
leaving hardly so much as a name

I'm just a lonely voyager
who on life's seas is tossed
my compass has been stolen
and my life-line double-crossed

going to die

I've been around for a few million years
and there's some tales that I could tell
if I had a mind, and I thought they would sell
but I won't waste my spleen
there's too much I've seen
and I know you people are too greedy and mean
to spend your time
on tales like mine
and that's why you're going to die

> going to die, you're going to die
> we could have been partners, you and I
> but now you're going to die

I let you play on my skin and in my hair
in my ears, and in my beard
and now I'm repaid in damage and pain
that have gone beyond my wildest fears
yes, for my kindness
I get nothing but death
rust in my blood and dust in my breath
and that's why you're going to die

come to my bed

day is dead
care is shed
and I'll sing you my song
if you'll come to my bed

> I know you came with another man
> but where is he in sight?
> wedded to variety
> and the healing power of night
>
> take your time
> take some wine
> spread your body
> over mine

hear me
I am no thane
I make no claim
I only wish to know you
well

> I believe something's owed by day
> but nothing's owed by night
> I too came with someone else
> and she's nowhere in sight
>
> but come the day
> I must away
> chances are
> to be taken

now day is dead
and care is shed
I'll sing you my song
if you'll come to my bed

one last kiss

snowdrops
raindrops
and I may be wrong
but I think I see some teardrops too
just a few
must be something to do with the time of year
spring tears

> sackcloth and ashes
> they're not for me
> I'm an off-hand man
> but I'm doing what I can
> to say I'm sorry
> so can't you give your lover one last kiss?
> one last kiss?

sunlight
lamplight
never shone bright enough
to highlight the treasure I had
I must have been mad
oh, baby, but you're in my limelight now
take a bow

> I know it's over
> my bags are packed
> I'm putting my pain
> on the very next train
> and I'm taking it away
> for a holiday
> where the dolphins play
> and I'm never bringing it back
> so can't you give your lover one last kiss?
> one last kiss?

no-one but you

No-one but you could nurse away my pain
No-one but you could love me like you do
I came in on a train
All unloved and barely sane
And I bless the day
And the crazy way
And the place where I met you

> No-one but you could cool my worry
> No-one could calm my hurry
> No-one but you could love me like you do
> No-one but you – you're my perfect lover
> You're the one I'll love for ever
> I have no-one
> And I need no-one
> And I want no-one but you

The young fields love to grow to the rains of spring
The cobwebs love to shine in the morning dew
Me, I love to sing
It makes me feel like a king
So here I sing
Of the love of a king
That loves no-one but you

No-one but you could rainbow through my rain
Or in my cloudy night like a star shine through
For every son there's a mother
For every lover, another
But none so fine
Sweet lover of mine
Or as beautiful as you

Lady Lovely & Mr Teddy Bear

come on, young lady, off to bed
or you'll turn into a sleepy head
it's after dinner and the sun's gone down
and you're the sleepiest little lady in town

> Lady Lovely, soft and fair
> hush, don't fret
> or you'll upset
> your Mr Teddy Bear

here am I – big, brown and strong
to lie beside you all night long
what more could a teddy bear do
for a lovely little lady like you?

tomorrow, if it doesn't rain
we'll go down to the woods again
we'll pick wild flowers and berries there
just Lady Lovely, and Mr Teddy Bear

make your own

when I was young
praises all were sung
of all that we would find
when we were grown . . .
perfect love shining bright on a golden throne

>we spun fine fantasies
>and wove them into song
>hoping to find some light some day
>but we were wrong
>we were wrong
>no such light shone
>and those who really wanted light
>made their own
>they made their own
>they had to make their own

our rainbow failed
just like the holy grail
yet still I see young people
every day
walking arm in arm down the same old way

>spinning out fine fantasies
>and weaving them in song
>well, such young people, I say to you
>you're wrong
>you're *wrong*
>write another song
>and if you want some light some day
>make your own
>make your own
>you'll have to make your own

strong boys, sweet girls
if you want a better world
make your own
there's no rainbow, no throne
no perfection except your own
make your own
you'll have to make your own

footprints in the snow

oh, what a story the seasons tell
a man is born when spring buds swell
in summer we bloom, in autumn we fade
in winter our cares for peace we trade
but we leave our footprints in the snow

> so that until spring people know
> that this way someone lived and loved
> grieved and gave
> and said hello
> and then goodbye

the more I learn and the more I live
the less I take and the more I give
when I die I hope to see
the earth receive me gratefully
but I'll leave my footprints in the snow

a game I had to win

there is no sun this morning
it's a cold and dirty day
and I wave goodbye
through the window pane
as I watch you walk away

    the perfume of your body
    still lingers on my skin
    and I wonder why
    I had to play your love
    like a game I had to win

you look so lonely on the street
getting smaller all the while
I long to see you
return my wave
and I long to see you smile

I feel an urge to call out to you
that I could be your ever-faithful lover
but I see my breath
on the window pane
has quietly frosted over

twilight

twilight is sailing down the river
hear and see, hear and see
and the woodland is aching for lovers
come with me, come with me

>the sun's going down
>with the wildlife sounds
>and the flowers are bowing their heads
>before the moon
>come play awhile with me
>on mother nature's knee
>and remember that we'll all be leaving soon

twilight is cool but rich in flavour
such wine is free, such wine is free
drink deeply while we still enjoy her favour
thank the trees, thank the trees

twilight will ebb and flow for ever
sailing well, sailing well
how long will she harbour us as lovers?
time will tell, time will tell

morning mist

remember when we kissed
in the gentle morning mist
as the spiders spun their webs across the dew
and the only stirring sounds
were the darkness going down
and feeling whispering between me and you?

> how I wish
> the gentle morning mist
> could last all day
> but the sun has cleared
> the morning mist
> away

I paid you what I owed
then I turned and hit the road
feeling like my debt had just multiplied
the sun began to rise
and I began to realize
that peace of mind is something a kiss can't buy

I'll keep the time we kissed
in the gentle morning mist
as carefully as I'd keep a priceless wine
for what's the life of a man
but a humble one-night stand
and a cellarful of songs, some poor, some fine?

just another goodbye song

You asked me for a love song
'Soft and gentle,' you said
And hard did I try
Sweet did I lie
But the words were all hollow and the melody dead
So here is the song that I wrote instead

> Just another goodbye song
> Just another farewell
> Just another 'So sorry, so long'
> New words to the tune that we know so well

All of life is a love song
So once I did believe
When I lived alone
And my time was my own
And I had never given but only received
Now in my will to such times I do leave

Life is all a goodbye song
Love is just the same
Now? Here to stay
Tomorrow? Away
Blown by no wind, and burned by no flame
And hardest of all, there is no-one to blame

the cipher

I move without motion
In a line without time
Effortlessly
For I am the art work
Evolving

I build my own monsters
I people my hell
And for those that make good
I make heaven as well
For these are the wages
of striving

I give you a cipher
The key to my gaze
Mark it well
For such is a lesson
In dying

earthly joys

(after William Dunbar)

As I did walk one June morning
Right early as the day did spring
I heard a bird in song exclaim

> All earthly joys return in pain
> In pain, in *pain*
> All earthly joys return in pain

Oh man, have mind, age follows youth
Death follows life with simple truth
Each bright day ends in night again

Where may health go but to sickness?
Where mirth, except to heaviness?
They with the most the most complain

Wealth, worldly glory, rich array
Are all but thorns laid in thy way
With envy green is conscience slain

Is ever May so fresh and green
That January comes not fierce and keen?
Fine seasons come, but none remain

Since earthly joys abide but never
Work for the joys that last for ever
Life not so is life in vain

blessed am I

Blessed is he who can say
'Blessed am I'
And tell no lie
And I have your love
Blessed am I

> Blessed is he in love with you
> *Blessed am I*
> Blessed is he who lives for you
> Sweet one, feel my heartbeat say
> *Blessed am I*

Blessed are the fish in the sea
And the birds in the sky
They cannot lie
But neither can they say
Blessed am I

Older we will grow
By and by
One day we'll die
But till then sometimes let's say
Blessed am I

old father time

who sometimes crawls and sometimes stands still
and sometimes spreads wings and flies?
who fades your flowers and puts lines on your skin
and steals the light from your eyes?
and who heals old wounds and mends broken hearts?
you've guessed? well, sorry no prize

> it's just old father time
> on his old railway line
> puffing down the centuries
> old father time
> on his old railway line
> can't you hear his whistle in the breeze?

who brings the seasons and takes them away?
whose puffing brings tears to the skies?
who brings our children, our sorrows and joys?
who brings our hellos and goodbyes?
and who brings an end to the longest of wars?
you've guessed? yes: surprise, surprise

The Asbestos Factory

It was during the summer before his final exams that Bennington Coggles began to hate the Prime Minister. His parents couldn't finance the vacation leisure Coggles coveted, and he was forced to take a job.

Several jobs, in fact.

The first was in a brewery. Coggles stood by a conveyor belt. His task was to remove broken bottles from the endless stream of screeching glass that goosestepped mesmerically past him. He stuck it for four days. Then the foreman accused him of inefficiency due to daydreaming.

'I *wasn't* daydreaming,' Coggles retorted. 'I was composing an ode.'

Three short jobs later he saw that the Olympus Stone Company had vacancies for manual workers. The pay was reasonable. Coggles applied and was taken on immediately. No references were asked for. This he attributed to his honest, serious countenance.

The work was hard. Heavy, dusty, unpleasant. From seven in the morning until seven at night he loaded corrugated roofing sheets on to lorries. The permanent workers in the factory were a sullen, uncommunicative lot. Humourless as Coggles himself; grey as the roofing sheets they handled. Since Coggles, with his unusually tall sinewy frame, was physically stronger than many of them, no-one teased him. He was let alone. Free to versify as he laboured. And to scribble the results into his notebook, while bolting his food, during the half-hour lunchbreak in the canteen.

Not until his second week, when he attended a talk given by a visiting union representative, did Coggles realize the Olympus Stone Company was an asbestos factory.

But why should this upset him?

Being a humanities man, he had only the haziest idea of what asbestos was and did. Furthermore, the union representative's concern was mainly to press for higher wages. And possibly, as an afterthought, for facemasks for the cutters, who worked indoors and tended to cough rather a lot.

Four days later, in the science column of the Sunday paper, Coggles read a detailed account of health hazards associated with asbestos. His complexion turned white, then yellowy green, and he was violently sick. When he returned from the toilet, trembling, and read the report again, he deduced not only that his risk of dying of cancer had multiplied enormously, but that this was largely the Prime Minister's fault. If the State paid its students a decent wage, he wouldn't have had to stoop to intellectually deadening labour in the first place. And if the Government were diligent and compassionate, instead of idle, incompetent and economically self-interested, the killer asbestos would have been outlawed long ago.

That was the instant in which Bennington Coggles began to hate the Prime Minister with such a fearful intensity that he lost weight and his few remaining friends as a result.

The following day he joined the Social Democracy Party.

By the age of thirty he had written 2,743 poems.

Many were overtly political. Some were thinly disguised catharses of his cancer neurosis. The asbestos latency period, he knew, could be twenty years or more. So he would *never* be safe. He was a walking timebomb, and his life became an excruciating struggle to take his ticking, twingeing symptoms to the Doctor as seldom as possible.

'How's the poetry going, Bennington?' the Doctor would ask kindly, on average once a month. 'Any luck with the competitions?'

No. Despite his command of literary jargon, Coggles had little talent. Few of his productions were not obsessively subjective. None had ever been successful.

His degree result was poor. Barely a pass. This he blamed on the Prime Minister. If he had been able to study during his last college summer, untortured by asbestos anxieties, he would, he was convinced, have done better in his exams. As it was, the Education Institution turned him down, and he was forced to take a clerical post in local government.

Here he was acceptably inefficient, but still his colleagues kept their distance. They were disturbed by his savage beaklike nose, the unkempt jungle of his auburn hair, and the haunted disdain of his orange-flecked green eyes.

'I got a tomcat wiv eyes just like wot that bloke has,' he overheard a typist say one day.

So none of his workmates visited the isolated cottage in which he ate, brooded, wrote and slept. His sole companion was a small yappy mongrel which arrived on the doorstep one evening, exhausted and starving, to offer its services as pest-control and garbage-disposal unit. It was a cross between Jack Russell and Pekinese, and it had extremely large testicles. Coggles called him Big Balls, but soon he was persuaded, by the Postman, to contract the name to Biggles, for fear of causing offence when summoning him in public places.

The Postman was a genial fellow, whose habit it was, as he cycled along the country lanes, puffing at a swan-neck briar pipe, to take benevolent potshots at the rabbits the local farmer had infected with myxomatosis. This he did with a double-barrelled shotgun pistol inherited from his ratcatcher father. Being himself the proud possessor of a mortgaged bungalow, the Postman was a supporter of the Prime Minister, and sometimes on Saturday mornings Coggles and the Postman would engage in warm debate on political issues, while Biggles strained to nip the Postman's ankles.

Biggles was happy with Coggles, and Coggles was less unhappy with Biggles. The unknown poet, despite his hatred of the Prime Minister, had a reasonable compassion endowment, and this he lavished, undiluted, on his dog. Lean beef was sacrificed, handsome new collars were purchased, and many long forays into the countryside were undertaken at weekends. In the summer, on a hot day, Coggles would stop for a chilled lager outside his local pub, and Biggles would beg for crisps from other patrons' children. It was a welcoming inn, with a friendly landlord, and Coggles would have liked to frequent it more often. The reason he didn't was the smoky atmosphere, which he knew, from reading the science column in the Sunday paper, would accelerate the rate at which asbestos cancer killed him.

In the country at large, the Prime Minister's policy of controlling the economy by unemployment had generated some resentment. But then the Prime Minister caused, fought and won a pointless war with a small, ill-equipped but unpopular enemy. This brought all the little shards of malice in the population into line with the Prime Minister's own massive malice, like iron filings regimented by a magnet.

Hence the Reactionary Party won the next election by a large majority, and the Prime Minister was authorized to cut public spending and increase unemployment yet further.

Prevailing opinion held that the average quality of life and the moral fibre and dignity of the nation were increasing handsomely. This view was premised on income statistics, holidays in Majorca, and sales figures for electronic washing machines. Actually, underlying the material improvement, there was an insidious moral decline. The structure of the welfare state itself, by decreasing the selective disadvantages of egoism and malice, and the selective advantage of compassion, was slowly moulding a populace dispositionally more selfish and savage than ever.

Meanwhile the Prime Minister went from strength to strength, and Coggles' detestation escalated.

Still, a minor Coggles victory was won when the Prime Minister's bill to reintroduce capital punishment was defeated. This defeat was hailed by television, and by the Sunday paper, as a victory for humanitarianism. In fact it was a temporary triumph for rational egoism, since the evidence clearly indicated that terrorist murders would be *increased* by the restoration of the death penalty. Coggles immediately wrote a poem to the effect that the Prime Minister would be *pleased* to see a rise in terrorist murders, since this would warrant an all-out war on terrorism, and thereby boost the Prime Minister's popularity yet again, in time for the next election.

But the Sunday paper, for the twenty-second time, declined to publish his verse.

Shortly after the capital-punishment debate, the public-spending axe fell upon the local-government office where Coggles worked, and he was made redundant. Since he had savings equivalent to a year's salary, he was at first ineligible for Welfare.

Three years and a thousand bad poems later, however, Coggles and Biggles were trapped in the Welfare Safety Net. Gone were new collars and lean beef for Biggles. Even Coggles' chilled lager gave way to an infrequent cheap brown ale. It was a harsh, joyless, futureless existence. Coggles' asbestos obsession and loathing of the Prime Minister became chronically ferocious. His features twisted into a permanent snarl. He would mutter to himself as he trudged through the village, collecting his meagre rations in an ancient rucksack.

Local people avoided him.

Children crossed the street when they saw him coming.

Only the Postman still spoke to him.

The following year, the Government cut the Safety Net benefits by ten per cent, in accordance with the Prime Minister's curious theory that the people the Government had disemployed would be better motivated to find another job if their lives were made even more unpleasant in the meantime.

In the autumn Biggles fell ill. His eyes were dull, his nose was dry, and his belly was swollen and tight.

'*Worms*,' said the Postman.

Coggles went to a chemist and bought some famous-brand worm pills which were so expensive that he went without meat for a week. Also, they did not work. So he went to a different chemist and bought some even more expensive pills. These did not work either. By now Biggles was unable to eat, and his belly was so swollen that he could hardly walk. In desperation Coggles ran to a public callbox and telephoned a veterinary surgeon.

Could be worms, the vet said. Difficult to tell on the phone. Couldn't Mr Coggles bring the animal in?

How much would that cost?

Quite a lot.

Could the vet possibly accept deferred payment?

Well, perhaps until the end of the month, he could. In this exceptional case.

Coggles wrapped Biggles in a towel, laced him into the ancient rucksack, and carried him the six miles into town. All the way, following the bus route, he chatted to Biggles, recited snatches of light verse, and assured the dog he would soon recover.

Because Biggles had had the worms so long, the vet diagnosed, and because of his age, he had developed intestinal complications. He could be operated on, but that would be extremely expensive. In any case, in his condition, he might suffer a heart-attack during the operation. The kindest solution in the circumstances was to put him to sleep straightaway.

And this would be relatively inexpensive.

Coggles could not weep, but he spent the next fortnight in shock. He shivered a lot, felt inexplicably cold, and found it difficult to eat. The Postman, noticing his distress, determined to cheer him up. One day he gave Coggles an old black-and-white television, since he, the Postman, had just bought a new colour portable for his wife's bedroom.

When the shock passed, Coggles found his hatred for the Prime Minister was vicariously murderous. He wished with lurid intensity that some terrorist organization would assassinate the Prime Minister. Sniper's rifle, car bomb . . . the method was unimportant, though his preference was that the Prime Minister should suffer considerable pain before expiring.

The campaign for the next election was now under way, and it was difficult to turn on the television without being exposed to the Prime Minister's pompous, snidely spiteful smile and vapid, patronizing platitudes. Once, when he switched channels, Coggles found himself in the middle of yet another harrowing documentary chronicling the appalling consequences of asbestos inhalation. He quickly switched again, to a mediocre thriller movie, but his mind was so bruised that he couldn't follow the story.

Most citizens who once might have been proudly working-class had become smugly middle-class. As their compassion atrophied, their egoism and malice quietly prospered. In their eagerness to purchase desirable residences and second cars for the wife, they were blind to minority sufferings.

But might not the unemployment plague infect *them*?

They happily deceived themselves into believing the contrary, the Social Democracy Party disintegrated, and the Prime Minister was returned with the biggest majority in history.

Welfare benefits were cut by a further three per cent, and as a result of a referendum, instigated by the Prime Minister, capital punishment was reintroduced.

Three months later, Coggles complained to the Doctor of dizzy spells, headaches and pains in the chest. The Doctor, to whom Coggles had cried asbestos wolf *ad nauseam*, diagnosed depression caused by the loss of Biggles, and prescribed company, activity and plenty of fresh air. Soon, though, the symptoms included fainting fits and bleeding from unexpected places. Extensive tests followed, and:

'I'm *sorry*, Bennington,' the Doctor said gravely.

Cancer?

Unfortunately.

Malignant?

Alas.

Terminal?

Infallibly.

Caused by asbestos?

Well, often associated, but . . .

Coggles was gladdened by the news. He felt as if a rubber band, which had been tightly stretched inside his head for sixteen years, had suddenly snapped. A pack of tarot cards, it seemed, had fluttered into a decisive formation, and he knew precisely what he must do before he died.

Only the means bothered him. And that he might fail in the attempt. This possibility began to torment him as his asbestos obsession had previously. The Doctor had given him a year to live, though, and . . .

Two weeks later he heard that he had won second prize in the National Poetry Competition. This was worth £1,000 and would be presented by the Prime Minister, whose enthusiasm for The Arts, and especially Literature, was proverbial. The occasion would be televised, so please could Mr Coggles be suitably smart?

Mr Coggles spent the next month perfecting his method. Like his poetry, this was not original. He got the idea from a mediocre thriller movie on television. From the Postman he borrowed the double-barrelled shotgun pistol and a box of cartridges. He needed these, he explained, because he'd been persecuted by rats since the severe winter following the death of Biggles. Then . . .

The great Prizegiving Day came.

Coggles arrived immaculately attired in a dinner jacket, crimson velvet bow tie and matching cummerbund bought specially for the occasion, on credit. None of the security men thought to examine the beautiful bouquet of purple and bronze chrysanthemums which he shyly hoped to present to the Prime Minister. Probably they couldn't conceive that a privileged prizewinner could be so ungrateful as to bear the Prime Minister any illwill.

After the first fanfare, the Prime Minister, sucking up the publicity like a leech ballooning on blood, delivered a not particularly short or comprehensible speech about the contribution of Literature to the cultural and, especially, the economic health of the nation. Then the first prize was given smoothly, and Coggles stepped forward.

Gaunt and pale, towering two heads taller than the Prime Minister, he leant forward and crisply whispered what he had rehearsed so often:

'Prime Minister, for what you have done to me, and to countless others, many yet unborn, I am going to kill you.'

He waited for the sickly smile to congeal into aghast realization, then thrust the chrysanthemums into the Prime Minister's face and pulled the string which fired both barrels of the shotgun pistol.

The Prime Minister's head blew off and an excited television commentator blurted that by Christ he couldn't believe such a bloody mess had come out of such a small amount of brains.

Coggles was overpowered (though he did not resist), detained, tried, and sentenced to death.

He refused to appeal. He was *not* insane, he insisted vigorously. He had performed a public service.

And the week before Bennington Coggles was due to be executed, he learned, from the front page of the Sunday paper, that a multinational pharmaceutical company had rush-released a magic bullet for all known malignant tumours. The treatment had been developed in secret, for commercial reasons, in accord with the enterprise economy.

Part V

LATER 1980s

crumbs of love

Sweet young thing
To you I sing
To you I offer my everything
Just give me some love
For a song or two
And I won't be in your way

> Give me some crumbs of your love
> Take what little I have
> I'll love you gently until you leave
> And I won't be in your way
> Give me some crumbs of your love
> And you'll see
> I won't be in your way

Time flies by
Old feelings die
So heed this older man's battle cry
Give me enough love
For my song or two
And I won't be in your way

Look at you
Cares so few
Cocksure with knowing where you're going to
Well, love me enough
For that song or two
And I won't be in your way

oh, love

Oh, Love
Wherefrom do you come? Where do you go?
Once I thought I did know
Oh, Love
I treated you like a sweet saxophone
That I could blow

> Oh, Love
> Don't pass me by
> Oh, Love
> Make bright my eye
> I know I've been a cold fish
> And I've broken all your rules
> But I'm older now, I know you're king
> And I'm happy to be your fool

Oh, Love
When I was young and green, you came my way
And with you I did play
Oh, Love
How could I use you like a ten-penny toy
I could throw away?

Oh, Love
I'll be your saxophone – I pray you, blow
How many tunes do you know?
Oh, Love
Blow me as snow on your mountain most cold
I'll melt and flow

Beautiful Jane

You were a child, so was I
When we swore we would love till we'd die
Looking back now, I can hardly believe
How someone like you could love someone like me

> Beautiful Jane
> Oh, beautiful Jane
> I wrote you this song to explain
> That I take the blame

So gentle and tender were you
The sweetest girl ever I knew
Yet I became restless, with my manhood to prove
With so little to give, and so much to lose

I saw you today from afar
And you looked happy, as young mothers are
With a child in your arms, and a sigh in your breast
In a moment of doubt that what turned out was best

rats in the soul

I was going to be
A hero with a halo of pure gold
I worked hard to improve my mind
And ride it beyond the world of time
And for all my pains, what happened to me?
I got rats in my soul

> While I dug out my hole
> Rats were climbing up my soul
> Now you can see
> What happened to me
> I got rats in my soul

Years ago, just any tolling bell
And I would burn to know for whom it tolled
But now I find I cannot care
I have no sympathy to share
It's all been eaten out of me
By the rats in my soul

Ask me, how does it feel
To be an unsung hero growing old?
Well, I'm not as rich as I might be
But I'm never short of company
Because a wonderful thing has happened to me
I've got rats in my soul

love is lonely

'Love is love is love is love'
I heard it yesterday
In some bar or maybe on TV
I don't know what it means and yet
It's made me want to say
Love is a thief that steals my dreams from me

> And love is lonely
> For love is only
> A one-off flower growing wild
> Love is lonely
> For love is an only child

Here am I in love with you
And lost for what to say
To you I'm just an old and faithful friend
I had my chances years ago
And I let them drift away
Thrown like a poor man's fortune to the wind

Love is what it means to see you
Hold your lover tight
Cling to him like ivy to a tree
Love is thinking such thoughts of you
All through long sleepless nights
So love is a thief that steals my dreams from me

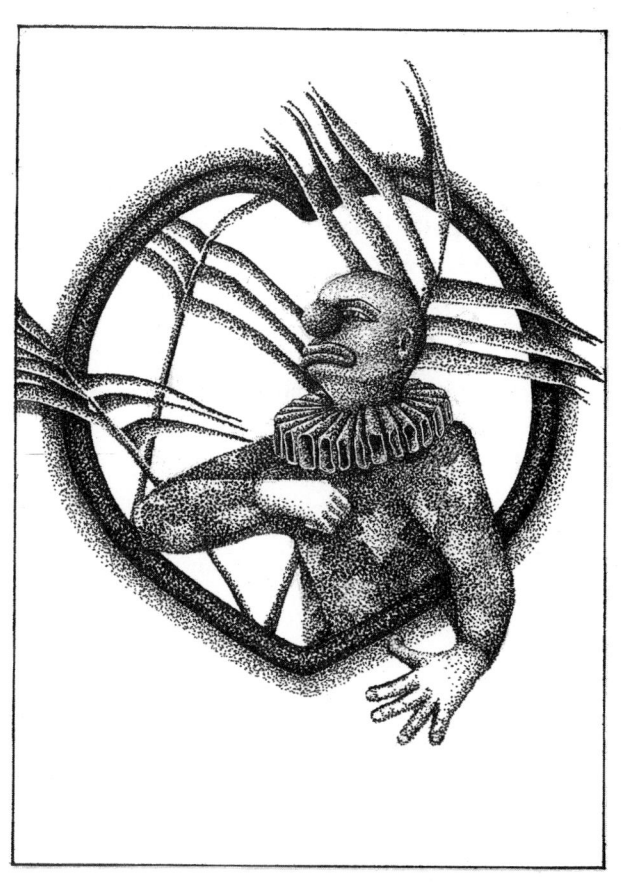

the stars shone

(after Robert Louis Stevenson)

The bright lights below from the city shone out
Through the windows of the houses and bars
While high overhead and all moving about
There were thousands of millions of stars

> The stars shone
> Like fairies that watched from above
> And the stars shone
> In the dancing waves of the sea
> The stars shone
> Their smile on the dawn of our love
> For the stars shone
> On a love that always will be

The Dog and the Plough and the Hunter and Bear
Swam brightly with the tears in your eyes
But the tears were for joy at the love that we shared
For a true love, once born, never dies

> Yes the stars shone
> Their smile on the dawn of our love
> For the stars shone
> On a love that always will be

the trees they did grow high

The trees they did grow high
And the leaves they did grow green
Many were the lovers
Who thereabout had lain
Would that such times
Could ever come again
For they were young then
And daily growing

The lovers brought forth children
Who brought forth children in their turn
And all the lovers' children
Had love's lessons still to learn
In about the woodland
On a bed of moss and fern
For they were young then
And daily growing

And all the lovers' children
Clustered thick upon the ground
To house their many children
They had to build a great new town
The woodland all was levelled
And the trees were all cut down
Thus love had put an end
To their growing

light a candle to the lonely

Most times I can't speak to you
I wear a mask all day
So heed me now if you ever will
I've shed my mask to say

> Light a candle to the lonely
> Act to harm no man
> Light a candle to each and every
> Beating heart
> Pass by no outstretched hand

I have no power to confess you
To clear you of your crimes
Just the echo of a sympathy
That sings in me sometimes

But I do not dare to ask you more
Than you may ask of me
In precious moments when the masks are down
We share our sympathy

don't fly away

Happiness
Is like a songbird that you can't caress
You must not touch it lest
It flies away
And love's the same
Another songbird you can never tame
Or ever teach the game
That you would like to play

> *Don't fly away, oh my pretty birds*
> *Stay here where you belong*
> If you even think such words
> You will not hear their song
> And they will fly away

Here am I
A lonely thinker with a misty eye
Watching clouds drift by
Expecting rain
For happiness
And love have left me in a wilderness
Full of emptiness
Till I can hear their song again

lonely to be lonely

Something's happening to me
There's a mole on the heart of my joy
And I ache for the world
Where you were a girl
And I was an innocent boy

> I'm lonely for
> The lonely roar
> Of the wind and the pounding sea
> I'm lonely to
> Be lonely with you
> And for you to be lonely with me

Now I live by the rules, my diary is full
My dreams are shallow and grey
And I long for the land
Where with time on my hands
I would write a new song every day

Do you remember a time when together we climbed
A clifftop overlooking the sea
And we loved in the rain
And we loved without pain
And swore we would always stay free?

But I cannot complain, I'm making my name
No time is the price that I pay
And I'll see it all through
Just so that with you
I can be lonely again some day

love let me down

Love is free
Like a wanton tree
That grows new leaves in spring
And teaches them to sing
Of the passion and the pleasure
That the summer long will bring
And the beautiful pain
Of the autumn rain
And the tasteful shades
Of the greens that fade
To yellows, reds and browns

>Oh, love, why did you let me down?
>Love, love, why did you let me down?

Love told me
That I must be
An ardent swain and true
That I must pay my dues
In passion and in pleasure
And in grief when I was used
And not to complain
When the pleasure brought pain
For pain, love said
Shows love is not dead
But only out of town

Now I'm a leaf
That's known much grief
And felt the autumn rain
The beauty of the pain
When the passion and the pleasure
Long since had bloomed in vain
A wind tore me
Right off the tree
And I shouldn't complain
For I feel no pain
I'm just lying on the ground
Slowly dying, on the ground

> Oh, love, why did you let me down?
> Love, love, why did you let me down?

Hannah's beautiful day

Hannah and me
Went down to the sea
One holiday summer's day
The day was new
And the sky was blue
And the waves all seemed to say

> What a beautiful day to be happy
> What a beautiful day to have fun
> What a beautiful day to be friendly
> And kind to everyone

Then Hannah and me
Had lunch by the sea
And the seagulls had lunch too
And the waves sang on
Their happy song
And the seagulls sang it too

Then Hannah and me
Went home for tea
Along the woodland path
Where a mischievous breeze
Was tickling trees
And making them seem to laugh

And Hannah and me
Had a wonderful tea
With Hannah's mum and dad
We ate cream buns
In the evening sun
And we sang 'cos we were glad

goodbye, young man

When I was a young man
Not so long ago
I knew there was nothing
That I didn't know
My world was a forest
I was Lord of the Trees
There was only one hero
And that hero was me

    Goodbye, goodbye
    Goodbye, young man that was me

And there in the forest
I lived with my friends
In the freedom of prison
And hours without end
And in that great forest
No breeze ever blew
No season of doubting
Shook the leaves that we knew

And young girls a-plenty
As fair as could be
Walked alone in that forest
With eyes bright for me
But I did not court them
For fear they would climb
Like a strangling ivy
On the trees of my time

One morning it happened
I arose with the dawn
A chill wind was blowing
My friends were all gone
And in the near distance
I heard the dread sound
Of chainsaws approaching
And trees falling down

harbour sounds

So far away is that morning
So far in space, far in time
And so far away
The waves and salt spray
And so far the lover
Who was so proud to be mine

>Harbour sounds, harbour sounds
>Boats unloading and crying seagulls, I hear
>Harbour sounds, harbour sounds
>I close my tired eyes
>And harbour sounds fill my ear

Farewell, magic morning
Farewell, cloudless blue skies
Farewell, farewell
The songs in the shells
And farewell for ever
The true love in those eyes

love or money?

Some people sing
About all that you don't need money for
Money, they say, can't buy love or happiness
And maybe it's partly true
But let me put it to you
What would you rather
A true love now
Or a billion dollars cash?

> Money, money
> Buys you milk and honey
> It can ease your worry
> Give you time to think and play
> Love or money?
> Me I'll take the money
> Take it somewhere sunny
> And give even money
> That love will come my way

Love is the mother
Of many a beautiful melody
Love is the screen where all sweet dreams appear
Love is many things
But has she ever paid for your guitar strings
Or your socks and shoes
Your union dues
Your breakfast or your beer?

No, there's nothing
In this world that you don't need money for
So goes life in the twentieth century
We've made a world of rain
That you can only leave on the gravy train
Where money's the key
And love is free
But never guaranteed

except sometimes when it's raining

listen, my pretty, as the blade meets the clay
though I'm just a gravedigger I am digging today
my rooms could be cleaner and my guests are all grey
but I've never yet heard them complaining
and I work like a trojan to brighten their stay
except sometimes when it's raining

> here's parsley for you
> and sage and thyme
> and rosemary too
> little sweetheart of mine
> for I love you
> as I love my signs
> except sometimes when it's raining

sometimes as I glide by the fringe of the sea
or take shade from the shade of an ancient oak tree
I hear nature's voices sing sweetly to me
and they save my old spirit from waning
and remind me how lucky I am just to be
except sometimes when it's raining

I return to my graveyard at the close of the day
for I'm just a gravedigger giving symbols away
a humble producer casting parts for a play
and there's only one part remaining
and if you'll come with me I'll love you always
except sometimes when it's raining

Appendix I

VERSE IN EDUCATION

In general, first, what is creative writing? By analogy with certain other words ending 'ive', such as 'promotive', creative writing ought to be writing which tends to create. Pornography? I would prefer 'created writing' or 'original writing', but 'creative' seems to have won the slot, so let's accept it, and tame it with a definition. My own, deliberately loose, definition of 'creative writing' is 'writing which could not have been written by someone else'. That makes virtually all writing creative, but recognizes that some writings are more creative than others. In these terms, anonymous sarky articles in the Sunday papers are less creative, while *King Lear* and *Ulysses* are more so.

Second, two possible reasons for not teaching (or stimulating) creative writing. *(a) there is always a danger of raising hopes,* and of subsequent disappointment. *(b) more politically, there is a risk of subversion* involved in any encouragement of creativity – not necessarily instant anarchy; but original writing (etc) requires original perception, which is of its nature iconoclastic.

Third, and I hope more persuasively, let's look at several reasons why we should encourage creative writing. *(1) catharsis;* the externalization and amelioration of personal problems and neuroses. As a sometime teacher of 'creative writing' I have encountered numerous students, particularly teenagers, more interested in having a sympathetic adult to talk to than in winning the Booker Prize. *(2) pleasure;* writing can be fun! The acquisition and exercise of new skills is satisfying. *(3) literary productivity;* one hopes to discover and nurture new talent, leading to enrichment of culture. *(4) social efficiency;* stimulation of creative writing can stimulate creativity generally, promoting a more dynamic approach to problem-solving . . . in work, life, love, whatever. What is creative writing, after all, but a nonstop caravan of problems and solutions? *(5) enhanced quality of life;* since success (in any problem-solving) is a self-image and motivation booster. *(6) **promotion of literacy;*** hence communication competence in all walks of language. The best writing says most with least words. If we teach a student to improve the signal/noise ratio in his/her poetry, some of that should (should!) carry over into the reports which that graduate will write years later as a permanent under-secretary.

My involvement with student writers intensified in 1986, when I was appointed to the Writing Fellowship at the Glasgow universities. My theoretical concern with how far it is possible and desirable to *teach* creative writing was sharpened by the HETE (Higher Education Teachers of English) Conference at Glasgow University in April 1988. What follows was focused by those two experiences, and nourished by an ongoing project to computerize a course of adaptable creative-writing teaching modules.

At the Glasgow conference a number of axioms were aired, some of which I believe are both true and important. With Philip Hobsbaum I agreed that the writing of poems, stories, plays, etc, is *just as important* as criticism in the teaching of English. But I go further, and argue that production of primary texts (novels, plays, etc) is *far more important* than production of secondary texts (commentaries, critical essays, and so on). The tree can flourish without the shadow; not the shadow without the tree. With Alasdair Gray I agreed that the value of writers' groups and classes is not necessarily to launch great writers. Just as the local tennis club very rarely breeds Wimbledon winners. That doesn't matter. Indeed, competent club players on a warm June evening are probably enjoying their game, and lives, much more than Becker on Centre Court.

With James Kelman I agreed that studying English (as usually taught in secondary schools and universities) is no qualification for doing or teaching creative writing. Imagine someone who had never driven a car trying to teach a learner. You don't have to be Prost or Mansell to instruct the novice, but you must have passed your own test. A more aggressive way of saying this: you can't fully understand X-ing unless you can X yourself. (It does not of course follow that if you *can* X yourself, you *do* fully understand X-ing.)

To complement my colleagues' axioms, I submitted that *talent cannot be taught*. Failure to accept this can have tragic consequences. In Somerset Maugham's *Of Human Bondage*: 'It was clear that the will to achieve could not help you and confidence in yourself meant nothing. Philip thought of Fanny Price; she had a vehement belief in her talent; her strength of will was extraordinary.' And by the next page Fanny has hanged herself. However, not all is lost. That talent cannot be taught does not entail that it cannot be educated. Furthermore, just as most people can be taught to pass their driving test, so can they be shown how to write a poem, construct a story, or plot a play. Also, however well anyone writes, he or she can be taught to write *better*. That goes for all of us, and a painstaking editor can make a bad book readable, and a good book excellent. One of the roles of the creative writing teacher is to *edit* students – to gently hold the mirror up to their imperfections.

So I think that, subject to the foregoing qualifications, creative writing *can* be taught, and I believe it *should* be a central component of any English course. But what about specifics?

The first problem may be: how to *motivate* students – to write a story, or improve a poem? Some have strong intrinsic motivation. Good for them. Others need, or want, goads and carrots. Such as? Provocation! Though only in certain cases. Possibly 'feminist literature is a contradiction in terms' – write a short story to prove the contrary. Praise! Admiration; recognition. Not necessarily on a cosmic scale, but the availability of sympathetic feedback may make the difference between a new poem being written and four lonely pints being downed in a gloomy pub. Sometimes encouragement works best through the sharing of woes, and several of my aspiring novelists were cheered to hear that my first novel, *McCandy*, was turned down by eighteen publishers before being accepted.

If the real possibility of publication does not exist, why not create it? Nothing is more unmotivating than to feel no hope of getting published. Therefore the birth of a new publication (class or college magazine, book/anthology, or whatever) will tend to generate new contributions. Alliterating in parallel with Parkinson: Poetry proliferates in proportion to the perceived possibilities of its publication. And money! 'Money is a good soldier, sir,' remarks Falstaff. (Today he might say: 'Money is a good publisher.') Other important things (like literary dignity) being equal, few incentives are more effective than money. For students, financial incentives can take the form of token payments for contributions to college magazines, or prizes in competitions. Competitions are healthy, I believe, often spawning works that otherwise just would not have happened, and in this regard such publications as *Writers' Monthly* and *Writers News*, which publicize literary competitions, can be useful teaching aids.

Motivation, especially in younger students, may exist in a rather vague and free-floating form. 'I want to be a writer' and 'I don't know what I want to write' are not contradictories. So when one asks a new group of writing students what kinds of writing they want to do, answers may vary from hardnosed specifics (Mammoth Sagas For The Women's Market, ET Scripts For Spielberg), to wider and in some ways more commendable ambitions such as:

'Poetry, I think.'

'How many of us have written a poem in the last week/month?'

Now the odd hand or two may flutter up, or lips purse expressively. But what if we continue the interrogation with:

'And how many of us have actually *read* a poem in the last month/year?' Here, in my experience, the glances lower shamefully, and feet scuff the floor. Poetry, it seems, is still generally held to be a Good Thing. The cachet of being a poet is durably desirable. Yet the ignominy of being caught going to the bother of actually *reading* poetry? Many students just wouldn't be seen dead . . .

That may be a fair comment on some of the offerings served up these days under the description 'poetry', in ever more slender volumes at ever less negligible prices. But from the point of view of *succeeding as a producer*, to not first serve some apprenticeship as a catholic consumer is inevitably suicidal. Given that premise, my teaching strategy (only one way of doing it) can be summarized:

ADMIRE, ANALYSE, IMITATE, FORGET, ORIGINATE.

Thus:

ADMIRE. Why imitate Jeffrey Archer, if you think his books

stink? (It may be his income you admire – but that's another problem.) My advice is: from the writing you admire, select some works worth emulating. Then:

ANALYSE. Chop it into manageable units. See how your model achieves his effects. And forget about critical categories; they aren't relevant here. (Others may analyse in terms of resonances, felicities, textualities, or whatever-elsies; but such concepts mean no more to the practising writer than . . . mermaids to a shipwright.)

IMITATE. Use your analysis to concoct something similar to your model. Keep his skeleton; substitute your own flesh. Never be afraid to imitate. Nobody will shoot you for it. Not until you are published. Even then, your notoriety will only sell more books. Seriously, anyone who doubts the creative value of imitation probably hasn't (so should) read Vasari's *Lives of the Artists* – just one short quote: 'Raphael then rid himself completely of the burden of Pietro's manner to learn from the work of Michelangelo a style that was immensely difficult in every particular; and he turned himself, as it were, from a master into a pupil once more.'

FORGET. No need to try! As life and preoccupations march on, our past admirations, analyses and imitations sink gradually from awareness, to decompose in our murky depths.

ORIGINATE. Here is the mystery. Sometimes it happens; often it doesn't. There is no guarantee that true origination will ever happen, but a virtual certainty that without the preceding stages it won't. Learning to write poetry (say) is like (or *is*) learning a second language. The ascent towards original utterances is similar. Some learners make it to the top; others do not. As to the psychology of inspiration, two books I remember finding instructive are Arthur Koestler's *Act of Creation* and, particularly, Anton Ehrenzweig's *The Hidden Order of Art*.

Now to practicalities.

For my own part, I have ended up more of a novelist than a poet, and even in the lyrical grip of a sunny May afternoon I am more likely to write/compose a new song than a more profound pure poem. Partly because when the computer goes to bed I would rather sing to a sweet guitar than wrestle with a silent pencil. So there's a limit to what I can offer any poet who is already both talented and accomplished. On a more basic level, I believe anyone incapable of writing a song lyric is unlikely to have written or ever to progress to great poetry. In any case, no grandiose claims are made for the activities suggested in Appendix II. They are elementary exercises which some teachers may find useful as starting points, to help students towards a foothold on rhythm and rhyme, and a taste of original creation.

Finally, in Appendix III, some suggestions are sketched as to possible interpenetrations and cross-fertilizations between verse and melody.

Appendix II

CREATING LYRICS

    1 COMPARE FIVE POEMS

    2 CLICHÉ-BREAKING

    3 BLANKED LEAR LIMERICKS

    4 BLANKS WITHOUT PICTURES

    5 LYRIC TITLES

    6 SONNETS

1 COMPARE FIVE POEMS

Upon the Snail

She goes but softly, but she goeth sure;
   She stumbles not as stronger creatures do:
Her journey's shorter, so she may endure
   Better than they which do much further go.

She makes no noise, but stilly seizeth on
   The flower or herb appointed for her food,
The which she quietly doth feed upon,
   While others range, and gare, but find no good.

And though she doth but very softly go,
   However 'tis not fast, nor slow, but sure;
And certainly they that do travel so,
   The prize they do aim at, they do procure.

I Hoped that with the Brave

I hoped that, with the brave and strong
   My portioned task might lie;
To toil amid the busy throng,
   With purpose pure and high.

The Wild, the Free

With flowing tail, and flying mane,
Wide nostrils never stretched by pain,
Mouths bloodless to the bit or rein,
And feet that iron never shod,
And flanks unscarred by spur or rod,
A thousand horse, the wild, the free,
Like waves that follow o'er the sea.

The Rainbow

EVEN the rainbow has a body
made of the drizzling rain
and is an architecture of glistening atoms
built up, built up
yet you can't lay your hand on it,
nay, nor even your mind.

Pippa's Song

The year's at the spring,
And day's at the morn;
Morning's at seven;
The hill-side's dew-pearled;
The lark's on the wing;
The snail's on the thorn:
God's in his heaven –
All's right with the world!

DISCUSSION

1 Do all five verses qualify as poetry?

2 Which poem/s do you prefer? Why?

3 Is there any one poem which you particularly dislike?

4 What sort of people wrote the poems? Men or women? Old or young? Happy or sad?

5 In which decade of which century was each poem written?

6 Choose one poem and write a page about why the poet wrote it, what it must have meant to him or her, and what it means to you.

2 CLICHÉ-BREAKING

Clichés have a nasty habit of being true. That's a cliché. But true. And potentially useful. If we're tired, or bored, a cliché can help us to stain the silence without stretching ourselves. Clichés can also serve as blinkers, to protect us from disturbing perceptions or reflections. Often useful, clichés can also be deadening, even dangerous: stifling the original freshness of perception on which creativity feeds. Refreshment of perception might come from a holiday or work stint abroad, or from an unexpected passionate romance with a filmstar. But it can also come from sticking the occasional subversive boot into the clichés we so often substitute for our own individual thoughts.

Sometimes clichés are broken by extension, or refinement. For example, the hack writes 'he stood still as a statue', but Cervantes writes 'he stood still as a draped statue, for the wind moved his clothes'. Alternatively, the cliché-breaker may improve his/her signal/noise ratio by suddenly changing categories. As in 'he stood still as a glass of stale cider'. It isn't necessary to be Shakespeare to be original. The original similes and sentences we spontaneously produce express the uniqueness of our characters, and spontaneity often begins and improves with practice. So . . .

"AS" SIMILES

cliché
>   (as) cool as a cucumber

compare
>   (as) cool as a non-paying customer

generate
>   NON-CLICHÉ SIMILES FOR THESE ADJECTIVES:
>   (as) meek / mad / dead / white / black / as . . . . . .
>   (as) brave / drunk / cold / hard / . . . / as . . . . . .

"LIKE" SIMILES

cliché

>He/she smokes like a chimney

compare

>He/she smokes like a derelict house burning down

generate

>CHANGING WORDS IN BRACKETS, AS YOU LIKE:
>He/she eats / drinks / sleeps like . . . . . .
>He/she snores / roars / looks like . . . . . .
>He/she sings / works / drives like . . . . . .
>The newlyweds got on like (a house) . . . . . .
>They came down on us like (a ton) . . . . . .
>Insults poured off him like (water) . . . . . .
>The bad news hit her like (a bolt) . . . . . .
>My love is like . . . . . .

PROVERBS, ETC

cliché

>A bird in the hand is worth two in the bush

compare

>A bird in the hand is likely to shit on your fingers

generate

>Empty (barrels) . . . . . .
>Out of the (frying pan) . . . . . .
>Once (bitten) . . . . . .
>Where there's (smoke) . . . . . .
>A(n) (Englishman's) (castle) . . . . . .
>Never look (a gift horse) . . . . . .
>And they all (lived) . . . . . .
>(Frailty), thy name is . . . . . .

3 BLANKED LEAR LIMERICKS

complete so they scan and rhyme:

There was a Young Lady whose chin
Resembled ... .
  So she ... .
  And purchased a harp,
And .... with her chin.

There was a Young Lady whose bonnet
Came untied when ....
  But she said, "I ....
  All the birds in the air
Are .... on my bonnet!"

4 BLANKS WITHOUT PICTURES

Complete the following limerick in your own style, paying reasonable deference to reasonable taste. Hillhead is the university district of Glasgow, and 'heavy' beer is the Scottish equivalent of English bitter. Feel free to substitute lager, etc.

> There was a duff pub at Hillhead
> Where the heavy was . . . .
>   Then a barmaid with mumps
>   . . . .
> And now the beer's . . . .

The next poem, entitled 'The Months', is by Christina Rossetti. Write out the verse and fill in the blanks – so the poem makes sense, rhymes nicely, and is pleasing to the eye and ear.

> January cold desolate;
> February all dripping . . . ;
> March wind ranges;
> . . . . . changes;
> . . . . in tune
>   To flowers of May,
> And sunny . . . .
>   Brings . . . . ;
> In scorched . . . .
> The storm-clouds . . .
> Lightning-torn
> . . . . . . bears . . . . .
> September fruit;
> In rough . . . .
> . . . . . must disrobe her;
> Stars fall and . . . . .
> In keen . . . . ;
> And . . . . . is . . . .
> And . . . . is . . . . . .
> In . . . . . December.

5 LYRIC TITLES

Set aside an hour per day for ten consecutive days. Pick a title from each group in turn, and write the following lyrics/poems:

DAY 1 FREE VERSE
      2 LIMERICK
      3 FREE
      4 HEROIC COUPLETS (4 beats)
      5 FREE
      6 BLANK VERSE (iambic)
      7 FREE
      8 SONNET
      9 FREE
     10 SONG LYRIC

Aim at between five and twenty lines. Write as quickly/spontaneously as you can within each day's form. Professional polish can be applied later, so first encourage your imagination.

DAY 1	ABSOLUTE CORRUPTION	ADONIS DESCENDING
	AGAINST NATURE	ALL THINGS WILL DIE
	BEAUTY IN DISTRESS	BEST BEFORE END
	BIGOTRY'S VICTIM	BLACK HOLES
DAY 2	BLACK WIDOWS	BLANK VERSE
	BLOOD SPORTS	BORED GAMES
	BY THE FIRESIDE	CHILD CRUELTY
	CLOSE ENCOUNTERS	CORPORAL PUNISHMENT
DAY 3	DEAF AND DUMB	DEATH IN LIFE
	DINOSAURS	DISPOSABLE NAPPIES
	EQUAL OPPORTUNITIES	FALSE REPORT
	FOR SHAME	FRAGMENTS OF REMORSE

DAY 4	FRIENDSHIP	FULL MOON
	GREENHOUSE EFFECTS	GUNS AND BUTTER
	HENS' TEETH	HERE'S HEALTH
	IRRATIONAL NUMBERS	JANUS
DAY 5	KISSING HELEN	LIFE HEREAFTER
	LIGHT AT MIDNIGHT	LONDON FATCATS
	LOVE IN A NUNNERY	LOVE LOCKED OUT
	MARRIAGE À LA MODE	MARY QUEEN OF SCOTS
DAY 6	MEETING AT NIGHT	METAMORPHOSES
	MIDNIGHT DEW	MY CLEAR-HEADED FRIEND
	NAKED APES	NASTY, BRUTISH AND SHORT
	NIGHT'S CARESSING GRIP	NOTHING WILL DIE
DAY 7	NUCLEAR POWER	PERSONAL REASONS
	PIPE DREAMS	POETIC PAINS
	ROBIN HOOD	ROTTEN TEETH
	SECRET LOVE	SELF-PORTRAIT
DAY 8	SEX ON CELLULOID	SLEEP AND POETRY
	SLEEPING BEAUTY	SMELLY WORDS
	STILL LIFE	SUNDAY MORNING
	THE BOTTLE OF KNOWLEDGE	THE DROWNED LOVER
DAY 9	THE EAVESDROPPER	THE FLOWER AND THE LEAF
	THE GREAT LOVER	THE HEEL OF ACHILLES
	THE POET'S MIND	THE POWER OF MUSIC
	THE SACRED WOOD	THE SPECTRAL HORSEMAN
DAY 10	THE WANING MOON	TIME TRAVEL
	TIME'S REVENGE	TOO LATE
	VISIONS OF SIN	WEDDED SOULS
	WOMEN AND ROSES	WOMEN'S MINDS

6 SONNETS

[A] The world is too much with us; late and soon,
Getting and spending, we lay waste our powers:
Little we see in Nature that is ours;
We have given our hearts away, a sordid boon!
This Sea that bares her bosom to the moon;
The winds that will be howling at all hours,
And are up-gathered now like sleeping flowers;
For this, for everything, we are out of tune;
It moves us not.—Great God! I'd rather be
A Pagan suckled in a creed outworn;
So might I, standing on this pleasant lea,
Have glimpses that would make me less forlorn;
Have sight of Proteus rising from the sea;
Or hear old Triton blow his wreathèd horn.

[B] When I have seen by Time's fell hand defac'd
The rich-proud cost of outworn buried age;
When sometime lofty towers I see down-ras'd,
And brass eternal, slave to mortal rage;
When I have seen the hungry ocean gain
Advantage on the kingdom of the shore,
And the firm soil win of the wat'ry main,
Increasing store with loss, and loss with store;
When I have seen such interchange of state,
Or state itself confounded to decay;
Ruin hath taught me thus to ruminate—
That Time will come and take my love away.
    This thought is as a death, which cannot choose
    But weep to have that which it fears to lose.

[C] O nightingale, that on yon bloomy spray
        Warblest at eve, when all the woods are still,
        Thou with fresh hope the lover's heart dost fill,
        While the jolly hours lead on propitious May,
     Thy liquid notes that close the eye of day,
        First heard before the shallow cuckoo's bill
        Portend success in love; O if Jove's will
        Have linked that amorous power to thy soft lay,
     Now timely sing, ere the rude bird of hate
        Foretell my hopeless doom in some grove nigh:
        As thou from year to year hast sung too late
     For my relief; yet hadst no reason why,
        Whether the Muse, or Love call thee his mate,
        Both them I serve, and of their train am I.

OVER TO YOU

1 The sonnets are, alphabetically, by Milton, Shakespeare and Wordsworth. Which is by whom? Why? Is any one sonnet somehow better than the others? Which rhyme pattern do you prefer?

2 What poetic devices, figures of speech and other technical tricks do the writers employ? Do the strictness of the forms and the slickness of the execution get in the way of the emotions expressed?

3 *EXERCISE*. Read each sonnet at least three times at intervals of at least one hour. Write down the first line of each sonnet. Wait two days. Then continue from one first line until you have completed your own fourteen-line sonnet.

4 Byron wrote: 'I never wrote but one sonnet before, and that was not in earnest, and many years ago, as an exercise – and I will never write another. They are the most puling, petrifying, stupidly platonic compositions. I detest the Petrarch so much, that I would not be the man even to have obtained his Laura, which the metaphysical whining dotard never could.'
   Do you agree? Would you rather be Byron than Petrarch?

Appendix III

WORKING WITH MUSIC

In *The Hidden Order of Art* Anton Ehrenzweig presents an analytical description of the creative process which – though it may not apply to everyone – has made profitable sense of my own creative throes, and which I have also found useful in helping student writers to overcome their problems.

Artistic creation, Ehrenzweig argues, happens in three identifiably distinct phases. First there is a neurotic, quasi-schizophrenic process, in which certainties have to be questioned, standards relaxed or even abandoned, traditional moulds fragmented, clichés of language and perception broken – all so that emotion and imagination may be liberated to see and hear, paint and write, make and record a work which is uniquely new.

Second comes a period of unshackled mania, during which (the old moulds and clichés lying shrivelling far below) the artist's creative juices flow with copious confidence, and the body of the new work is born. Now the artist is like a child who, previously nervous about climbing such a precarious ladder, feels free for a while to run riot in the attic of wonders.

Of course no-one can or should revel madly aloft for ever, and the third stage is one of descent, literally of come-down: usually into weariness, often into dissatisfaction, hopefully into a fruitful degree of self-criticism, and sometimes into deep disorientation and potentially dangerous depression. This latter part of the cycle is less fun to be in, but it is an essential part of the deal, and anyone who fails to undergo it, or who endeavours to avoid it, is unlikely to become an artist of stature. This is because, inevitably, not everything produced during the flights of euphoria is definitively perfect, or even of any objective value at all. Critical discernment is vital to the revision and improvement of individual works, and also to the evolving maturity of the artist's creative career.

Ehrenzweig's analysis is very fecund, and of course I am failing to do it full justice in this thumbnail sketch from memory. The divers uses to which it might be put include: (a) explaining – sympathetically, and perhaps prophylactically – why, judged from the hidebound, cocksure ground floor of bourgeois mores, the lifestyle of so many artists, writers and composers seems shambolic; (b) their above-average proneness to alcoholism, drug-addiction, and faster forms of suicide; (c) why so many 'mature adults' (seem to?) lose the abundant creativity they experienced/enjoyed in their teens and early twenties. And so on.

I began the present appendix with Ehrenzweig because I believe a skilful use of music can help budding poets and songwriters to recognize, survive and progress above the neurotico/schizoid level, which some might otherwise mistake for an impenetrable ceiling. Very young children know no barriers, but teenagers (after years of 'Do this', 'Don't do that', 'Never start a sentence with "And"' . . .) are full of inhibitions. At once rebellious and obedient, arrogant and timid, they frequently lack the confidence to write with the spontaneity they possessed ten years before. One way of loosening the bonds of conformity wrapped round them by parents and teachers is to play their favourite rock music so loud that they can *feel* it, and encourage them, spurred by and in rhythm with the music, to write or type out, as fast as possible, whatever comes into their heads. The nominal point of the exercise may be to start a diary, or write a letter to a friend, but the underlying objective is to achieve a free-flowing stream of consciousness. Students, here, should be urged to disregard punctuation, and to let their sentences surge on of their own momentum – as long as possible, and with no matter what connectives.

Once some results have been achieved with pop music they know well, try something similar with evocative/dramatic classical pieces, such as Grieg's 'Hall of the Mountain King', or Berlioz's 'Fantastic Symphony'. Once everyone's consciousness is copiously streaming, an instructive variation may be:

'Now stop writing, close your eyes, and just *listen.*' When the music is over, they write down all they can remember of what they thought/imagined while it was playing. Of course abreaction is not of itself art (as an alcoholic psychiatrist once assured me with vindictive loathing), and no immortal masterpieces are likely yet to have been produced. But that's beside the point. What we want here is to kindle a taste for seeing, feeling and thinking in less fettered modes, and to enhance the novice writer's self-image with the realization that:

'Even I am well able to coin striking, provocative and unique turns of phrase.'

A second desirable result is a body of fresh material which then can be reflected upon, analysed, related to the writers' biographies, regurgitated, punctuated into greater readability, and possibly made the basis of something more closely approaching Art. Expand a dream sequence into a coherent story; take ten lines/phrases and rearrange them into a free-verse 'poem'; from what you have written, choose the five best song titles – what sort of songs would they be, and who would sing them?

For students motivated to attain some creative-writing proficiency, above and beyond sheer self-expression and fun, now might be the moment to begin the cycle outlined in Appendix I:

ADMIRE, ANALYSE, IMITATE, FORGET, ORIGINATE.

And the admiring might commence with something like the *Compare Five Poems* activity suggested at the beginning of Appendix II.

Doubtless certain anarchists will disagree, but I believe all great and even professionally competent poets and songwriters are versatile practitioners of scansion and rhyme, even if they don't always use them – a bit like proportion and perspective in the visual arts. Hence the emphasis in Appendix II on demandingly strict forms such as limericks and sonnets. If ever you are approached by a student with rhymeless poetry so intense and abstruse that you wonder despairingly whether here is a new Ezra Pound, or a self-regarding charlatan peddling twaddle, try giving him or her a limerick to write or complete. Should the result fail to scan, it's a fair bet you've got twaddle.

(Even if the limerick scans perfectly, alas, it doesn't follow that you haven't got twaddle.)

Technical expertise is not a sufficient condition, but it is necessary. Necessary, that is, to all lyric writers who hope to leave a little more behind them than 'Rock Me Baby' and 'The Moon In June'. Therefore, I think, apprentice songwriters (eg) should work hard not only at their songs themselves, but at practising sonnets too. Just as training boxers not only spar in the ring, but also do road-running, circuit workouts, and so forth.

'But look here!' the protest will be voiced. 'I've done all that. I've completed my limericks, rendered my couplets perfectly heroic, got my sonnets quintessentially Shakespearean, but I still can't write a song!' 'Why not?' 'I can't write music!' 'Can you play an instrument?' 'No!' 'Do you ever sing?' 'Well, um . . . Sometimes in the bath, yes. But only when no-one is listening.'

Here, then, is another inhibition well worth scotching, and one tactic is to begin in private with a tape recorder – preferably with a thumb-control microphone, and absolutely not in the bath! Just as almost all people can speak, though millions cannot sign their own name, so, though few can notate crotchets and quavers, virtually all of us can create simple melodies.

Try it. Take your tape recorder to a peaceful place, either your bedroom at dead of night or a rock by a stream in the hills by day, and quietly sing on to it some of the lyrics in this book. Wait a day. Look at the lyric/s again. Can you remember the tune/s you sang? Sure? Sing them on to the tape again. Compare today's recording with yesterday's. Identical? Differences? Improvements? Now do likewise with an original lyric of your own.

'But I haven't got any lyrics of my own!' 'Why not?' 'I don't know! I've done everything you said – and I'm sick of limericks, I've written umpteen free verses, I'm fed up to the gills with sonnets, and after all that . . . '

Music, with a bit of luck, can now help us out again. Get a friend, ideally someone who can play an accompanying instrument such as guitar or piano, to play and hum (*la-la*; no words) on to a tape the tunes of some songs he knows but you don't. If you don't have such a friend, record some songs from a foreign radio station: in a language you don't understand. What you now have are the musical halves of songs crying out for new lyrics. So get busy!

Listen to the melodies frequently. Immerse yourself in the mood and emotional qualities of the music. Sketch on paper the shapes of the verses and refrains: number of lines, and patterns of line-end rhymes. Now hum along as you listen. If you find any words and rhymes popping up in your mind, jot them down. If you don't, leave it for a day and try again. Keep at it until the components of a new lyric begin to pursue you, seemingly with a will of their own, and won't let you alone till you have captured them on paper, and integrated them into perfection.

But now you have a fresh problem: a new lyric that is difficult to think away from the old tune, which belongs to someone else. Solutions include: (a) give up; (b) acquire permission to use the old tune – as Paul Anka did with the French original of 'My Way', which must have made the composer very delirious, at least financially; (c) wait until you think you have forgotten the old tune, and then reset the lyric to your own new tune – but be sure then to compare your new tune with the supposedly forgotten one, just in case they are embarrassingly similar; (d) pass your new lyric on to a composer who does not know which older melody was the basis of your lyric.

This brings us to collaboration.

Many fine lyricists can't compose wonderful melodies, and vice versa. The very nature of song makes sharing of creation both possible and often desirable – as legally reflected in the normal fifty-fifty split between words and music in song rights and royalties. Though some (including myself) would argue that, as with all artistic endeavour, the pinnacles of songwriting greatness will only be scaled by the best efforts of a unitary consciousness, it is undeniable that Tom's lyric sung to Dick's melody frequently sounds more pleasing and memorable than if it were set to Tom's own tune. In learning situations this natural complementation of talents can be of enormous value – for example, when two individually alienated students, each apparently incapable of completing anything at all, come to realize what a productive songwriting team can be born of their harmonious co-operation. Not all such teams will become as Rodgers–Hammerstein or Lennon–McCartney, but a few will, and for others the therapeutic, educational and social benefits of joint endeavour, enhanced respect for others, etc, will far outweigh any financial or direct career advantage.

If collaboration is a Good Thing, which comes first: lyric or melody? Whenever I work with another songwriter, the procedure invariably is that a lyric by me is set (often including alterations to the verse structure) by him or her. But this is probably at the relatively literary end of the songwriting spectrum, and songwriters specializing in dance music, rhythm-and-blues, and so on, are more likely to start from a musical phrase, or even a beat or bass riff, and then mix in lyrics to taste. However, there really are no rules, and it could just as well happen that *both* lyric and melody come first: in that a mature lyric and self-contained tune are introduced to one another, as it were by a dating agency, and then interactively adapted until they click.

Thus was my own first song written. I was sixteen, had just left school to pre-empt being expelled, was washing dishes in a Wimpy Bar, and had mentally penned a rather gauche lyric entitled 'A Year From Now'. But I couldn't compose a tune for it that didn't sound too like Bob Dylan. Mike Maran, at seventeen, was spiriting Special Grills to the tables in the same Wimpy, and in his head had created a suitably unDylan-like melody. So we fudged the two together, and bingo: a mediocre first song, but for both of us a blockade of inhibitions had been broken.

We still sometimes write together, but increasingly, throughout our twenties and thirties, we have written our own complete songs – which of itself proves nothing, but is at least consistent with the view that the most mature and accomplished songs any individual writes are likely to be organically integrated emanations of his/her uniquely perceiving mind. Why? No-one, to my knowledge, explains the matter more lucidly than Schopenhauer:

'The characteristic nature of the song in the narrowest sense is as follows. It is the subject of the will, in other words, the singer's own willing, that fills his consciousness, often as a released and satisfied willing (joy), but even more often as an impeded willing (sorrow), always as emotion, passion, an agitated state of mind. Besides this, however, and simultaneously with it, the singer, through the sight of surrounding nature, becomes conscious of himself as the subject of pure, will-less knowing, whose unshakable, blissful peace now appears in contrast to the stress of willing that is always restricted and needy. The feeling of this contrast, this alternate play, is really what is expressed in the whole of the song, and what in general constitutes the lyrical state.

'In this state pure knowing comes to us, so to speak, in order to deliver us from willing and its stress. We follow, yet only for a few moments; willing, desire, the recollection of our own personal aims, always tears us anew from peaceful contemplation; but yet again and again the next beautiful environment, in which pure, will-less knowledge presents itself to us, entices us away from willing. Therefore in the song and in the lyrical mood, willing (the personal interest of the aims) and pure perception of the environment that presents itself are wonderfully blended with each other. Relations between the two are sought and imagined; the subjective disposition, the affection of the will, imparts its hue to the perceived environment, and this environment again imparts in the reflex its colour to that disposition. The genuine song is the expression or copy of the whole of this mingled and divided state of mind . . .

'The lyric form is therefore the easiest, and if in other respects art belongs only to the true genius who is so rare, even the man who is on the whole not very eminent can produce a beautiful song, when in fact, through strong excitement from outside, some inspiration enhances his mental powers.'

In those terms, I believe, a truly beautiful song is apt to erupt in a matter of moments, lyric and melody already crystallized together. But for this to be possible the poet/songwriter must have cultivated both poetic and musical abilities. So I urge aspiring lyricists to also learn to sing (which requires correct breathing, and inspiration is breath), and to acquire at least strumming competence on an accompanying instrument such as piano or guitar. And, just as I remain suspicious of the brow-furrowed self-styled poetic marvel who cannot rhyme, I'm a little dubious too about a poet who cannot sing.

For dishonesty hides more easily behind the words on a printed page than between the same words sung with feeling.

Suggested Reading

Too often, when in Waterstone's I browse through the latest overpriced slender volumes of 'contemporary poetry', I feel that here is matter monochroically fuzzy, ineptly unmusical, confected by persons who covet the cachet of 'writer' but lack the requisite talent. Self-expression is not of itself art, and many new poems, which it would be exciting to receive from a student, do not ipso facto merit publication for sale to the public. Having declared that lack of interest, I leave the specifying of worthy contemporary poetry to others better versed.

Some longer-ago poets, of greater potential value to songwriters, are: William Blake, Robert Burns, Samuel Taylor Coleridge, John Donne, William Dunbar, T. S. Eliot, Gerard Manley Hopkins, A. E. Housman, Wallace Stevens, and W. B. Yeats. Also Baudelaire and Rimbaud, especially if one can read them in French.

Novels I suggest in three categories. First, those written by and/or about songwriters. Here I can offer my own *McCandy* (comedy following the frustrations of an ambitious young songwriter in an Old University Town) and *The Wishdoctor's Song* (darker comedy, and something of a period piece). In the same class: *The Favourite Game* and *Beautiful Losers*, by Leonard Cohen; *The Myrtle and Ivy* and *The Sinner*, by Stuart MacGregor; and *Espedair Street*, by Iain Banks. Second, some novels I was influenced by, during the years when I wrote most songs: John Barth, *The Floating Opera*; Thomas Berger, *Little Big Man*; Mikhail Bulgakov, *The Master and Margarita*; William Burroughs, *The Naked Lunch*; Ralph Ellison, *Invisible Man*; John Fowles, *The Magus*; Hermann Hesse, *Steppenwolf*; Gabriel García Márquez, *One Hundred Years of Solitude*; Michel Tournier, *The Erl King*; Nathaniel West, *The Day of the Locust*. Third, 'totemic' novels – certain to be read and re-read for centuries to come. Among the few twentieth-century British novels in this league are: Robin Jenkins, *Fergus Lamont*; James Joyce, *Ulysses*; Malcolm Lowry, *Under the Volcano*.

Finally, my two most constant inspirations. Shakespeare – supreme dramatist, and a master songwriter too. (C.f. *Twelfth Night*, *The Tempest*, *Midsummer Night's Dream* . . .) And Schopenhauer. One can't fully understand his metaphysics without first mastering Kant, but many of Schopenhauer's shorter essays (in *Parerga and Paralipomena*) are very accessible. Consider also chapters 37 and 44 of Volume II of *The World as Will and Representation*. Bryan Magee's *Schopenhauer* is an excellent introduction.

Index of titles by page

9	*Introduction*	57	prayer from the trees
		58	god's eye
14	not for you	60	the men in the forest
15	light and laughter	62	a handful of sand
16	the monday boy	64	lady of the wheels
17	the ballad of the galleon	66	songs unsung
18	spiders	67	graven faces
19	sleepy eyes	70	still I must be gone
20	still the winds		
21	thistledown	71	*A Song for Atlantis* (story)
22	grotto motto		
22	I love Elizabeth	84	the brightest smile
23	the garden	85	drowning
24	the gondolier	86	real hard case
25	the last winter	87	the emperor and the geisha girl
26	the railway	90	crazy delight
27	sold for a song	91	weed's warning
29	the night is kind	92	sober serious man
30	mistress, go gaily	94	soapsuds in my gravy
31	water lady	96	the very first song
32	crazy days	97	from the heart
33	pledge of love	98	sitting there
34	go your way	99	McCandy's chorus
		100	on my way
36	*White Christmas* (story)	101	a memory framed for ever
		102	looking forward to summer
40	playback	104	the eye
42	leaves	105	a sailor's plight
44	ice	106	take me away
45	the title	107	rainy eye
46	god's tears	108	moonlight shines
48	cargo	110	close your eyes
49	the serpent caper	111	the swallows are leaving
52	the omen		
53	a maid's lament	112	*Philosopher's Mother* (story)
54	perfect moment		
55	the swineherd's lament	116	here I am

117	beautiful pirate	164	*Verse in Education* (appendix)
118	going to die		
119	come to my bed	169	*Creating Lyrics* (appendix)
120	one last kiss		
121	no-one but you	170	Compare Five Poems (exercise)
122	Lady Lovely & Mr Teddy Bear	170	Upon the Snail (Bunyan)
124	make your own	170	I hoped that with the Brave (Brontë)
125	footprints in the snow	170	The Wild, the Free (Byron)
126	a game I had to win	171	The Rainbow (Lawrence)
127	twilight	171	Pippa's Song (Browning)
128	morning mist	172	Cliché-Breaking (exercise)
129	just another goodbye song	174	Blanked Lear Limericks (exercise)
130	the cipher	175	Blanks without Pictures (exercise)
132	earthly joys	176	Lyric Titles (exercises)
133	blessed am I	177	Sonnets (examples & exercise)
134	old father time		
		180	*Working with Music* (appendix)
135	*The Asbestos Factory* (story)		
		187	*Suggested Reading*
144	crumbs of love		
145	oh, love	190	*Index of titles by alphabet*
146	Beautiful Jane		
147	rats in the soul	192	*About Black Ace Books*
148	love is lonely		
150	the stars shone		
151	the trees they did grow high		
152	light a candle to the lonely		
154	don't fly away		
155	lonely to be lonely		
156	love let me down		
159	Hannah's beautiful day		
160	goodbye, young man		
161	harbour sounds		
162	love or money?		
163	except sometimes when it's raining		

Titles by alphabet

About Black Ace Books, 192
Asbestos Factory (story), 135

ballad of the galleon, 17
Beautiful Jane, 146
beautiful pirate, 117
Blanked Lear Limericks (exercise), 174
Blanks without Pictures (exercise), 175
blessed am I, 133
brightest smile, 84

cargo, 48
cipher, 130
Cliché-Breaking (exercise), 172
close your eyes, 110
come to my bed, 119
Compare Five Poems (exercise), 170
crazy days, 32
crazy delight, 90
Creating Lyrics (appendix), 169
crumbs of love, 144

don't fly away, 154
drowning, 85

earthly joys, 132
emperor and the geisha girl, 87
except sometimes when it's raining, 163
eye, 104

footprints in the snow, 125
from the heart, 97
game I had to win, 126
garden, 23
go your way, 34

god's eye, 58
god's tears, 46
going to die, 118
gondolier, 24
goodbye young man, 160
graven faces, 67
grotto motto, 22

handful of sand, 62
Hannah's beautiful day, 159
harbour sounds, 161
here I am, 116

ice, 44
I hoped that with the Brave (Ann Brontë), 170
I love Elizabeth, 22
Index of titles by page, 188
Introduction, 9

just another goodbye song, 129

Lady Lovely & Mr Teddy Bear, 122
lady of the wheels, 64
last winter, 25
leaves, 42
light a candle to the lonely, 152
light and laughter, 15
lonely to be lonely, 155
looking forward to summer, 102
love is lonely, 148
love let me down, 156
love or money?, 162
Lyric Titles (exercises), 176

maid's lament, 53
make your own, 124
McCandy's chorus, 99
memory framed for ever, 101
men in the forest, 60
mistress, go gaily, 30
monday boy, 16
moonlight shines, 108
morning mist, 128

night is kind, 29
no-one but you, 121
not for you, 14
oh, love, 145
old father time, 134
omen, 52
on my way, 100
one last kiss, 120

perfect moment, 54
Philosopher's Mother (faction), 112
Pippa's Song (Browning), 171
playback, 40
pledge of love, 33
prayer from the trees, 57

railway, 26
Rainbow (Lawrence), 171
rainy eye, 107
rats in the soul, 147
real hard case, 86

sailor's plight, 105
serpent caper, 49
sitting there, 98

sleepy eyes, 19
soapsuds in my gravy, 94
sober serious man, 92
sold for a song, 27
Song for Atlantis (story), 71
songs unsung, 66
Sonnets (examples & exercise), 177
spiders, 18
stars shone, 150
still I must be gone, 70
still the winds, 20
Suggested Reading, 187
swallows are leaving, 111
swineherd's lament, 55

take me away, 106
The Wild, the Free (Byron), 170
thistledown, 21
title, 45
trees they did grow high, 151
twilight, 127

Upon the Snail (Bunyan), 170

Verse in Education (appendix), 164
very first song, 96

water lady, 31
weed's warning, 91
White Christmas (story), 36
Working with Music (appendix), 180

About Black Ace Books

Crumbs of Love is our first title. The second is *An Enlightened Scot*, by Aylwin Clark – the life of Hugh Cleghorn, student and friend of Adam Ferguson. 'It is the great value of Miss Clark's book,' writes Nicholas Phillipson, in his foreword, 'that she shows us an enlightened mind in the making.' A hardback of 352 pages, with 16 photographic plates, *An Enlightened Scot* is priced at £19.95. If you can't obtain it from your local good bookshop, please order it direct from us. (£19.95 per copy includes packing and UK mainland postage.)

Black Ace Books began in 1991. One motivation may be conveyed by the following horror story. ONCE A JOLLY NOVELIST determined to go electronic. Picture his delight: to find his new London Publisher was using the same text composition system as himself. Called Telos, it had been written in Edinburgh by Mike Ryan, then of Digital Publications. A wonderful system, so: *Whoopee*, thought the Novelist. No compatibility problems here! 'My disks, correctly coded, are ready to output to bromides,' he proudly informed the Publisher. 'How much will you give me for them? Half the saving is said to be fair,' he added politely, imagining the cost of needlessly re-typing 250,000 words must be daunting to any Publisher not a complete idiot. Alas:

'Your disks are of no value to us,' said the Publisher. 'However, send us a set anyway, and we'll use them to output proofs.' 'What would you do with those proofs?' asked the Novelist cautiously. 'Send them to the People's Republic of China,' replied the Publisher, 'to get your text re-keyed correctly.' Kindly preferring to think his Publisher more likely crafty than certifiably insane, the Novelist next advised his Editor to advise his Production Department to travel the world swiftly and replicate themselves out of their own genes incessantly. Henceforth things could hardly have deteriorated, but so indeed they did. And when the Novelist, many months later, received his first proofs back from China, via central London, peppered with more new errors than could credibly have been achieved by a blind chimpanzee on a typewriter, he swore a not wildly silent oath that ever after he would possess the means to publish, if need be, his own work to his own satisfaction.

On the brighter side, we can now do it. For ourselves, and others too. In 1993–4 our list will expand to include new fiction, and paperback reissues of quality novels which conglomerate publishing has allowed to go out of print. Details from: Black Ace, Ellemford, Duns, TD11 3SG, Scotland.